DREAMWORKS
TROLLHUNTERS
TALES OF ARCADIA
FROM GUILLERMO DEL TORO

WELCOME TO THE DARKLANDS

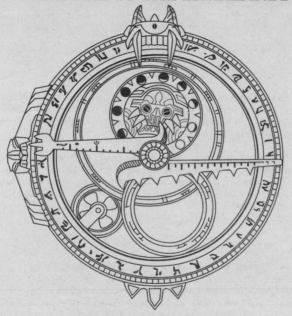

Written by Richard Ashley Hamilton

Based on characters from DreamWorks Tales of Arcadia series

Simon Spotlight

New York   London   Toronto   Sydney   New Delhi

SIMON SPOTLIGHT
An imprint of Simon & Schuster Children's Publishing Division
1230 Avenue of the Americas, New York, New York 10020
This Simon Spotlight paperback edition December 2017
DreamWorks Trollhunters © 2017 DreamWorks Animation LLC. All Rights Reserved. All rights reserved, including the right of reproduction in whole or in part in any form. SIMON SPOTLIGHT and colophon are registered trademarks of Simon & Schuster, Inc. For information about special discounts for bulk purchases, please contact Simon & Schuster Special Sales at 1-866-506-1949 or business@simonandschuster.com.
Cover design by Nick Sciacca. Interior design by Nick Sciacca.
Manufactured in the United States of America 0518 OFF
10 9 8 7 6 5 4 3 2
ISBN 978-1-5344-1288-0 (hc)
ISBN 978-1-5344-1287-3 (pbk)
ISBN 978-1-5344-1289-7 (eBook)

PROLOGUE
HEXILE

Gunmar the Black howled.

He howled in confusion, unable to tell day from night in this strange new realm. He howled in pain. Ice-cold winds whipped against his body—a body born in the fires of war. And he howled in defeat. Victory had been snatched from his grasp, just as Gunmar had been snatched into these dark lands.

Gunmar forced himself to stand. His hooves nearly slipped on the glowing green rock beneath him, but he found his balance.

Never again will I be brought to my knees, Gunmar promised himself.

He looked out at the Darklands with his single burning eye and watched his army start to appear around him. One by one, thousands of Gumm-Gumm soldiers arrived in flashes of blinding white light. They, too, crashed against the barren landscape, as Gunmar had done mere seconds ago. They, too, fell over with vertigo and shivered against the sudden cold.

Gunmar turned his horned head upward and saw the portal through which he and his army had been thrown. Killahead Bridge sat atop a jagged stone peak. Its arch shimmered with magic as more Gumm-Gumms plummeted into the Darklands.

Gunmar squinted his eye and stared through the portal. He glimpsed the distant surface world on the other side, as well as the enemy who had just banished him from there.

"Deya," said Gunmar with a low growl.

Deya the Deliverer stood guard at the other end of Killahead Bridge. Her silver Daylight Armor was battered and dirty from weeks of combat, but still unbroken. She planted her broadsword into the battlefield, a grim look of finality in the Trollhunter's eyes. Even across the immeasurable space that separated them, Deya's message was clear: *this war is over.*

"No!" Gunmar shouted.

He sprang into the air and climbed the peak toward the bridge like a wild animal. Gunmar's claws tore into the rock. He pulled himself higher, dodging the Gumm-Gumms that still fell out of the portal and past him. His body heaved, and his glowing blue veins pumped with energy. But Gunmar did not stop. He closed in, never taking his eye from Deya.

With only a few feet left between Gunmar and the Trollhunter, Deya reached up to her side of Killahead.

"No!" Gunmar yelled again, fangs gnashing in anger.

Deya's fingers closed around the Amulet embedded in the top of the bridge. Gunmar leaped toward her. His massive legs propelled him across the remaining distance.

"NO!" Gunmar shouted one last time.

But he was too late. Deya removed her Amulet from the bridge a second before Gunmar reached her. And the portal to the surface lands closed.

Gunmar's body hurtled through the now-empty air and collided with Killahead Bridge, reducing it to rubble. The inert fragments of the bridge then began to vanish around him, just as the portal had disappeared before his very eye.

Wrenching open his jaws as far as they could go, Gunmar the Black unleashed his most awful howl yet. The primal scream echoed across the Darklands for quite some time. When his wail finally faded, Gunmar looked down the peak to his army. The Gumm-Gumms all stared back at their fallen king, each too frightened to even blink under their heavy metal helmets.

"My son," Gunmar whispered, his throat raw. "Where is my son? Where is Bular?"

Unsure of how to respond, the soldiers looked at one another. Some shifted nervously, their weapons and armor clanking in the awkward silence.

"My lord," called a voice from below Gunmar.

The crowd of Gumm-Gumms parted, and a muscular, orange-skinned Changeling stepped forward. He swept his cape to the side and gave a slight bow in Gunmar's direction.

"Speak, Kodanth," said Gunmar to the Changeling. "For the information your *Impure* spies bring has always proven valuable."

"The last I saw of mighty Bular, he was slashing

most valiantly through the Trollhunter's forces, along the southern front," said Kodanth. "Might I suggest you question your general stationed in that vicinity?"

Gunmar fixed his glare upon a particularly large Gumm-Gumm whose body was decorated with stripes of war paint, and said, "The south was your assigned area."

"Y-yes, my lord," stammered the striped general.

"Then what news of my son?" demanded Gunmar.

"F-forgive me," answered the general after a long pause. "But Bular, he . . . deserted us!"

"What did you say?" Gunmar asked quietly, his eye narrowing into a flickering slit.

"That Krubera turncoat, AAARRRGGHH!!!—he switched sides and began fighting *with* the Trollhunter, not against her," explained the Gumm-Gumm. "Bular met AAARRRGGHH!!! on the field of battle, and they fought fiercely. But the traitor struck a lucky blow. He broke off part of the horn from Bular's crown."

The general pointed to his own right horn to indicate what had happened and then said, "Bular clutched his wound and fled before the Trollhunter placed her Amulet in Killahead Bridge and sent us here to—"

Gunmar landed powerfully before the general. He flexed his right arm, forcing strands of pale energy from his pulsing veins. The energy weaved together, taking shape and forming the Decimaar Blade in Gunmar's grasp.

"My son is no coward," said Gunmar, holding his arcane sword in front of the general.

More wisps of energy crawled off the blade and up the horrified Gumm-Gumm's face, until his eyes glazed over like mirrored chrome. The once-proud general stood unmoving and unfeeling before Gunmar, reduced to a mindless slave.

"Find the nearest abyss and throw yourself into it," Gunmar said matter-of-factly.

The entire army watched as the general did as he was told. Gunmar then stalked forward, pointing the Decimaar Blade at all of them. The Gumm-Gumms inched back in fright.

"My son is no coward," Gunmar repeated.

"Of course not," said Kodanth, stepping away from the others. "Bular's courage and bloodlust are second only to your own legendary—"

"Aah!" cried an unfamiliar voice, interrupting Kodanth.

Gunmar looked down and raised his hoof. He had just stepped on a hooded Troll who was far, far too scrawny to be a Gumm-Gumm.

"Mercy!" said the Troll from under his cloak. "Please, I beg of you! Grant me mercy!"

"I am not known for my mercy, stranger," uttered Gunmar.

He made his Decimaar Blade vanish in a cloud of mist before grabbing the Troll. As Gunmar dragged him bodily into the air, the Troll's hood fell back, revealing six frightened, blinking eyes.

"I recognize you," said Gunmar. "You're the Trollhunter's companion. The talkative one with his snout always buried in a book."

"Yes," answered the six-eyed Troll, his heart pounding. "Although I suppose my brother, Blinkous, has now inherited my library. I am Dictatious Galadrigal, at your service."

"You?" spat Gunmar as he tossed Dictatious back to the ground. "Serve me?"

Dictatious's body rolled to a stop at Kodanth's

scaly, orange feet. The Changeling sneered and said, "Only *I* advise Gunmar the Black! Gunmar the Vicious! Gunmar the Skullcrusher!"

Kodanth gestured to two Gumm-Gumms, and they immediately raised their axes over Dictatious's head. Satisfied, Gunmar turned his back on them and lumbered away.

"Send this six-eyed scum straight to Gorgus," Kodanth ordered.

"Wait!" Dictatious hollered, holding out all four of his arms to halt the Gumm-Gumm's axes. "Strike now and your only chance of leaving the Darklands dies with me!"

Gunmar stopped midstep and looked back over his shoulder. Seeing his single, livid eye, the two Gumm-Gumms immediately lowered their axes, sparing Dictatious for now.

"How could a fool like you ever get us out of this hopeless place?" asked Kodanth.

Still on his knees, Dictatious ignored Kodanth and instead addressed Gunmar.

"With all due respect, my Dark Underlord," he began. *"Drog respa sulk respaluk."*

"Even the word 'hopeless' isn't void of hope,"

Gunmar said to himself, translating Dictatious's last phrase.

"Ah, I see your mastery of Trollspeak is as sharp as your sword," said Dictatious, slowly getting to his feet. "One as unworthy as I would never *dream* of advising you. . . ."

Dictatious gave a smirk only Kodanth could see. The Changeling fumed in quiet outrage.

"But where some might see the Darklands as an inescapable death sentence, my six eyes see only *opportunity*," Dictatious continued. "For I know all too well how the Trollhunter and her ilk think. Let them believe they have won!"

Feeling braver now, Dictatious approached Gunmar, gesturing grandly at their dismal surroundings with his many hands.

"While they grow old and weak and mingle with those pathetic humans, you shall make the Darklands your kingdom," said Dictatious. "Where nothing grows, you shall build an unstoppable empire."

A smile spread on Gunmar's scarred face, despite the cold ache in his bones.

"Where others would never dare venture, you shall

bide your time, marshal your forces, and double—no, triple!—your already limitless strength," Dictatious went on, his voice building with each new word. "Where only death and despair lurk, you shall call out to your surviving son. And together, Bular the Brutal and Gunmar the Black shall once again storm the surface world and bring forth—"

"The Eternal Night," said Gunmar, finishing the thought as Dictatious knew he would.

For the longest time the only sound in the Darklands came from the frigid wind. Every single Gumm-Gumm held their breath and watched Gunmar, but none more intently than Kodanth and Dictatious.

"Kodanth," began Gunmar, breaking the silence.

"Yes, my lord?" Kodanth answered, beckoning those two Gumm-Gumms to raise their axes over Dictatious once again.

"Take the ten best battalions, find a secure location, and begin construction immediately on my new throne room," Gunmar ordered. "Dictatious will stay with me and explain how I might still commune with my son."

"Yes, my lord," said Kodanth through gritted teeth.

"And Kodanth," Gunmar added when Kodanth started to leave. "From this moment forward, you will also address me as 'Dark Underlord.' I find that a title befitting my majesty."

"As you wish, my lor—" Kodanth began, then halted. "That is . . . my Dark Underlord."

The Changeling cast a spiteful look at Dictatious, who winked back at him. Kodanth departed in a huff, his cape flapping as he strode past the bowed heads of several soldiers . . . including one named Skarlagk.

Skarlagk stood apart from the other Gumm-Gumms. Her mane had been shaved into a Mohawk that crested like a wave between her horns. She wore a quiver full of spears across her back. When Skarlagk finally lifted her eyes, she looked upon Gunmar not with awe or terror—but with hatred. He was close enough for Skarlagk to crush with her powerful arms. But she knew this wasn't the time to strike. Not yet.

"Tell me, sire, have you ever heard of a Fetch?" asked Dictatious, his voice fading as he and Gunmar walked away together. "It's a compact portal, far too small to allow a fully grown Troll to pass through. But it may be large enough to send messages to your son—as well as *other* little items to and from the surface world. And I believe we can construct these Fetches from the very rock found in the Darklands. . . ."

After Gunmar and Dictatious left, Skarlagk unfastened a satchel at her side and removed an old, weathered Gumm-Gumm skull. She held it to her own and said, "Soon, Father."

Skarlagk returned the skull to her satchel and struck out in the direction opposite from Gunmar. And for centuries, no living thing ever walked across this end of the Darklands.

Until . . .

CHAPTER 1
UNWELCOME

Jim Lake Jr. entered the Darklands alone.

The Trollhunter's black-and-red Eclipse Armor protected him from the cold, but not from the faint echo of his friends' voices. Looking back over his shoulder, Jim saw the rebuilt Killahead Bridge. Even though the portal under it had already closed, he could still hear his teammates on the other side, calling out to him.

"Jim!" yelled Toby from the surface world.

"Master Jim!" Blinky's voice carried into the Darklands. "What have you done?"

Jim took a deep breath and kept walking, trying to ignore them. But the Trollhunter's next step faltered, when he heard one more distant voice.

"Jim, come back!" cried Claire. "You don't

have to do this by yourself! We can figure this out together!"

Jim wanted nothing more than to run back to the bridge, reopen the portal, and return to the warm safety of Heartstone Trollmarket. He wanted see Toby's braces-filled smile again. He wanted to fist-bump all four of Blinky's Troll hands. And more than anything, Jim wanted to look into Claire's eyes. He wanted to tell her that he was okay, that deep down all this was for her—and her baby brother, Enrique, who had been stolen into the Darklands months ago.

But the Trollhunter didn't do any of that. Jim forced himself to tune out Claire's plea. He marched farther across the Dead Plains, until he reached a cliff. Standing at the edge of the precipice, Jim looked out on the endless expanse of the Darklands. His disbelieving eyes beheld towering rock structures that intersected at odd angles, a low black sun that cast a sickly light over everything, and a mind-bending maze that seemed to stretch into infinity.

The engravings in Jim's armor pulsed with red power. A split second later, the Sword of Eclipse appeared in the Trollhunter's hand. The black sword shimmered as Jim affixed it magnetically to his armored back.

"Get ready, Gunmar," Jim said out loud, even though he couldn't see a single sign of life anywhere around him.

Jim knew that somewhere down there, in the twisted heart of the Darklands, Gunmar the Black waited for him. And that when they finally came face-to-face, only one of them would survive the encounter. But Jim couldn't worry about that just yet. Before he could take on Gunmar, the Trollhunter had to find someone else.

Jim cupped his hands around his mouth and called out, "Enrique!"

Even though he projected as loud as he could, Jim's voice hardly seemed to carry over the dead, flat air in the Darklands.

"Um, remember me?" Jim continued. "It's your sister's favorite study buddy—Jim! Just, uh, gurgle if you can hear me!"

Jim waited for a response, but none came.

"Of course it wouldn't be that easy," Jim muttered to himself. "Looks like I've gone from being Trollhunter to *Baby*hunter."

Jim took a step, then stopped. His brow furrowed as he thought about what he had just said.

"Um, that came out wrong. I mean, who actually hunts babies? Other than, y'know, Gunmar and his Changelings. Maybe I should go by something a little more appealing, like . . . Baby*finder*? Babyrescuer? Babysaver? Yeah, Babysaver. That's way more appropriate. . . ."

Jim trailed off, a sense of isolation starting to creep in before adding, "Aaand I'm already talking to myself less than five minutes into the Darklands. Way to keep it together, Lake. . . ."

He looked over the edge of the cliff and wondered how he was going to climb down it. Jim suddenly found himself wishing he had bothered to pack a few supplies before jumping haphazardly through Killahead Bridge. He figured that stuff like a rope or compass or bottled water—or, heck, even a meatloaf sandwich—would've been kinda helpful right about now.

Maybe the Amulet could have guided Jim to a safer path, just as it had guided him ever since he found it months ago, in the Arcadia Oaks dry canal. Jim still couldn't believe how an Amulet created by

Merlin—yes, *that* Merlin—had passed to Jim from the previous Trollhunter, Kanjigar, just as it had passed to Kanjigar from Deya centuries before that.

But the Amulet wasn't of much use to Jim now. He had had to leave it back on the other side of Killahead Bridge. That was the only way to make sure the portal would reopen for Jim when he returned.

If I return, Jim thought darkly.

He looked down at the empty space over his heart where the Amulet usually ticked—where it had unlocked new weapons for Jim, like the Eclipse Armor. Like the Sword of Eclipse. Like the . . .

"Glaives," Jim said to himself, getting an idea.

He held his hands by his sides, and two curved blades—the Glaives—magically appeared in his palms. Using them like a pair of pickaxes, Jim lowered himself down the side of the cliff, like a mountain climber going in reverse. As he descended, Jim's mind couldn't help but wander. Each time he sunk a Glaive into the rock, another recent memory flooded into the Trollhunter's head.

KA-SHUNK!

Jim thought of the hurt looks on Claire's,

Toby's, and Blinky's faces as he locked them out of the vault in Heartstone Trollmarket, which held the ruins of Killahead Bridge.

KA-SHUNK!

He remembered inserting the final Triumbric Stone—a shard of Gunmar's missing eye—into his Amulet and reading the incantation that then appeared across its surface: "For the doom of Gunmar, Eclipse is mine to command!"

KA-SHUNK!

Jim recalled how the Amulet then turned Jim's armor from silver to ebony before magically reassembling Killahead and opening the portal. Even now, Jim still felt that stomach-churning sensation from when he had stepped through the swirling passageway and into the Darklands.

KA-SHUNK!

He wondered what would happen when his mom, Barbara, woke up from the spell that made her forget Jim was the Trollhunter. Would Draal honor his oath to protect her? *Could* he even protect her? After all, Jim wasn't worried about another attack from enemies like Strickler or Angor Rot. He was more concerned about how his mom's heart would likely break when she discovered her only son had now gone missing.

KA-SHUNK!

The Trollhunter mourned AAARRRGGHH!!! The soft-spoken Krubera Troll had saved Jim countless times, just as he had aided Kanjigar and Deya before him. But AAARRRGGHH!!! gave his life to save his friends, and now the gentle giant's mossy body had been turned to solid stone. In AAARRRGGHH!!!, Jim and the others hadn't just lost a teammate. They'd lost a friend.

Jim pushed away all those painful thoughts as he finally reached the bottom. He stowed the Glaives back inside the onyx plates on his thighs and scanned the dim surroundings.

That Changeling nursery has to be around here somewhere, Jim thought to himself. *If I find the nursery, I find Enrique. And if I find Enrique, then I can find my way back home to Claire, Tobes, Blinky, Mom, and everyone else who doesn't want to murder me.*

Jim shook his head in another attempt to clear his friends' faces from his brain. The Trollhunter had committed to taking on this mission alone. That was the only way to make sure those close to him would never be in danger again. Jim had just lost AAARRRGGHH!!! He wasn't about to lose someone else he loved.

Turning a corner, Jim stepped into a clearing, and his blood froze. A Gumm-Gumm at his post stood before him, leaning against a wide ax that looked corroded from ages of neglect. Jim was about to reach for the Sword of Eclipse on his back when he noticed something. The Gumm-Gumm wasn't moving. He hadn't even reacted to Jim's presence. In fact, the Gumm-Gumm almost looked like he was . . .

"Asleep," Jim whispered to himself in relief.

The Gumm-Gumm snored softly under his helmet. Jim tiptoed around the sentry, careful not to wake him. He had just crept behind the Gumm-Gumm's back, when another fierce wind blew across the Darklands. The gale loosened some gravel on a stone shelf over Jim's head. He watched with dread as the little bits of rock fell and clinked against the Gumm-Gumm's helmet.

Rousing with a start, the Gumm-Gumm stood bolt upright and yelled, "Who goes there?"

Jim cringed behind the guard's broad back, still

unseen. Once again, he tried for his sword, but the metal plates on his armor tapped together as his arm moved.

The Gumm-Gumm spun around and searched the space behind him. Fortunately, Jim jumped before the Gumm-Gumm could spot him, managing to stay behind his back. The Trollhunter timed his footfalls to land with the Gumm-Gumm's and kept out of his line of sight.

"If that's the Scorned or one of her rebels, come out to face me," the Gumm-Gumm growled. "And the end of my ax!"

Jim didn't move a muscle. Hearing nothing else, the Gumm-Gumm huffed in satisfaction. He leaned against his battle-ax and dozed off once more.

The second Jim heard the lazy lookout's snore return, he padded away as quickly—and as quietly— as he could. It was only after he was out of earshot that Jim remembered to breathe again. He exhaled visible clouds in the chilly air and shivered as he found himself in front of a labyrinth.

"I wonder if this Eclipse Armor could unlock a blanket for me," Jim joked to himself.

All of a sudden, Jim felt warmth against his back.

At first, he half believed that maybe the armor *had* given him a blanket. But when Jim turned around, he saw that the heat had nothing to do with him. It came, instead, from the large flying fireball that hurtled out of the darkness and toward Jim like a comet.

"WHO ARE YOU?" demanded the fireball. "WHO ARE YOU???"

Jim pulled the Sword of Eclipse off his back, held it in front of his body, and hoped like crazy that this new armor was fireproof. . . .

CHAPTER 2
GOOD MOURNING, TROLLMARKET

Piles of ancient scrolls and books of Troll lore sat open and unread on the large reading table in Blinky's library. The sounds of construction rang from outside as Trolls repaired the damage caused by Angor Rot's recent attack on Heartstone Trollmarket. But, otherwise, the library remained still and empty . . . until a tiny black dot appeared in the corner.

The dot quickly grew from a pinprick into a wide tear through time and space, causing the scrolls and books to flutter with a rush of wind. A voice was heard from the floating circle of shadow and said, "One! Two! Three! PUSH!"

A moment later AAARRRGGHH!!!'s stone body slid out of the black hole and into the library. Toby,

Claire, and Blinky followed, shoving their petrified friend into the corner. NotEnrique, however, reclined lazily on top of AAARRRGGHH!!!'s head, snacking on a sock.

"That's the spirit," NotEnrique went on. "Ya two fleshbags ain't so weak when yer put your backs into it!"

Toby and Claire shot the little Changeling a dirty look before they collapsed with exhaustion. Toby's round belly heaved as he caught his breath, while Claire wiped the sweat from her brow and tucked a blue lock of hair behind her ear.

"And . . . I used to think . . . ," Toby said between gulps of air. "That my wingman . . . was heavy . . . before!"

"At least moving AAARRRGGHH!!! gave us something to do," said Claire. "I don't think I could've handled staring at Killahead Bridge for another second . . . just hoping for Jim to come back through it."

She raised her Shadow Staff and made the black hole shrink and disappear altogether. It had taken Claire some practice, but she had gotten the hang of her new weapon. By opening these shadow portals and jumping through them, Claire could teleport to almost anywhere she wanted in the blink of an eye—anywhere except the Darklands.

Blinky shut his six eyes and nodded in agreement with Claire, but said nothing. Normally, he could speak at length on any subject. In fact, his brother, Dictatious, used to tease Blinky about never shutting up when they were younger. But that was a long time ago, before Dictatious mysteriously disappeared at the Battle of Killahead Bridge. Losing AAARRRGGHH!!!—and now maybe Jim—had left Blinky unusually speechless.

NotEnrique finished eating his sock and used AAARRRGGHH!!!'s smooth back as a slide. He landed on his tiny cloven feet and hiked up his diaper.

"Well, I'm bushed," said NotEnrique with a yawn. "Time to grab a pint at the Glug Pub. *Adios*, suckers!"

NotEnrique tossed them a wave over his shoulder as he strutted toward the library's exit. But Claire extended her Shadow Staff and hooked him by his diaper. She lifted the feisty little Changeling into the air so that they were now at eye level.

"Oi! What's the big idea, sponge-face?" NotEnrique said. "This's cruel and unusual, is what it is!"

"No," said Claire, leaning in closer to NotEnrique. "The 'big idea' is that you aren't going anywhere until we *all* figure out a way to help Jim."

NotEnrique pawed at the Shadow Staff and said, "What's that gotta do with me? I hardly even knew Jim. I mean—Jim who? Never heard of 'im!"

"Let's see if I can refresh your memory," said Toby as he got to his feet.

Toby reached into the back of his sweater vest and pulled out his Warhammer. Thanks to a Troll gravity curse, the massive mallet hit like a ton of bricks, yet weighed less than a feather. Everything about the Warhammer seemed beyond cool to Toby—from its long metal handle to its spiked crystal hammerhead. In fact the only thing *not* cool about the Warhammer was how Toby couldn't find a better holder for it than his sweater vest.

"Jimbo went into the Darklands to find Enrique—the *real* Enrique," Toby explained impatiently. "And since you were the shape-shifter sent here to impersonate Claire's baby bro, it's only fair that you play a part in Jim's rescue mission!"

NotEnrique gulped when Toby held the Warhammer up to his pug nose and added, "Unless you want to play a game of Changeling piñata?"

"I . . . suppose the pub can wait," mumbled NotEnrique.

"Super," said Claire. "Now, how can we open Killahead Bridge and go after Jim?"

She looked around at the many books stuffing the library shelves. Blinky had inherited thousands of volumes of Troll history from Dictatious and had only added to the collection in the ensuing centuries.

"The answer has to be in here somewhere," Claire continued. "Toby, you start checking *Gringold's Grimoire* while I review *Axle's Forbidden Almanac* and . . . and . . ."

Claire trailed off. Her shoulders sagged, as if she had suddenly run out of steam.

". . . and who am I kidding?" Claire finished so quietly, the others could barely hear her.

"Claire," Blinky finally said in a soft voice. "We both know that only the Trollhunter may open the portal to the Darklands. There is, regrettably, no way for us to follow him."

"Then maybe there's still something we can do to help him from here," Toby said, a determined look glinting in his eyes. "I still have that Fetch and—"

A buzzing ringtone interrupted Toby. He, Claire, and Blinky all looked at NotEnrique, who pulled a cell phone out of his diaper and started texting back.

"Wait a minute," Claire said. "Is that *my* cell?"

"Mmmaybe," NotEnrique winked.

"I'm gonna kill you, you green piece of—" Claire threatened before Blinky held her back with all four of his arms.

"Really, NotEnrique," said Blinky. "Must you be sending text messages now, of all times? Have you no respect for the sacrifices made by the Trollhunter or his compatriots?"

"All right, all right, don't get yer suspenders in a twist," said NotEnrique while he stuffed Claire's cell back into his diaper. "I'll just catch up with Draal later."

Claire tried to attack him again, but Blinky held her in place.

"Whoa! Whoa! Whoa! Slow your roll," Toby said to NotEnrique. "Draal was texting you?"

"If ya can call it that," NotEnrique answered. "He can barely type with that mechanical arm of his."

"But what did he say?" Blinky asked. "For that matter, where in Gizmodius's name *is* Draal?"

"Camped outside that surface hospital, keeping an eye on the Trollhunter's mum," said NotEnrique as he casually inspected his own fingernails. "Only now he says she's left the hospital and is headin' back to her house. Well . . . what's *left* of it, anyways . . ."

"Great Gronka Morka!" Blinky exclaimed. "Barbara was supposed to remain in the hospital for another day, at least! The lingering effects of the memory charm have likely left her quite confused. If she returns to her home and finds that it's been destroyed by Angor Rot—and that Jim has gone missing—"

"That's not gonna happen," Toby interrupted, hefting his Warhammer over his shoulder.

"If we can't help Jim, then we'll help his mom," said Claire. "It's what he would want us to do."

Now motivated into action, Blinky hurried over to the reading table. He examined two scrolls at the same time with his many eyes and said, "Very well.

You three convene with Draal and intercept Barbara before she sees too much and reverts into a state of severe shock!"

"Oh yeah?" said NotEnrique. "And what're ya gonna do—stay here and stare at statue-boy over there?"

Blinky sighed heavily and turned from NotEnrique to AAARRRGGHH!!! Toby poked NotEnrique in the ribs with his Warhammer. The little Changeling rubbed his side and averted his eyes, regretting what he had just said.

"I've already wasted enough time feeling sorry for myself," Blinky replied. "Now I must honor my friends' sacrifices in the only way I know how: hours upon hours of intensive library research!"

His six eyes welled with emotion as he looked up at AAARRRGGHH!!!'s stone face. Blinky smiled and said, "It's what *he* would want *me* to do."

"Eh, still sounds boring to me," NotEnrique said under his breath before Claire grabbed the tuft of fur on his back and yanked him out of the library.

"Hey!" hollered NotEnrique. "Watch me scruff!"

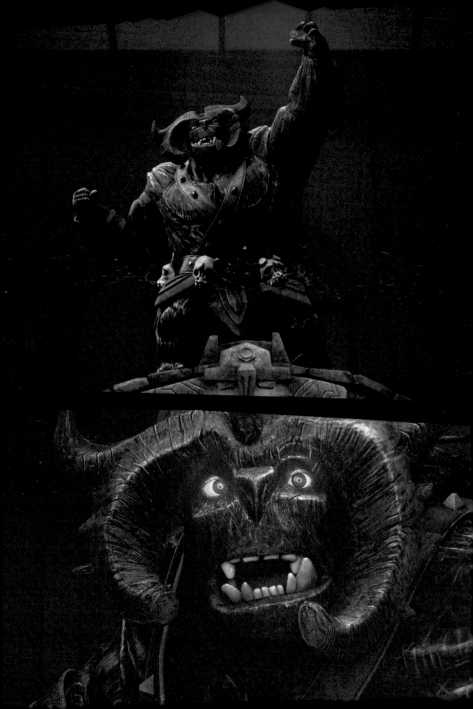

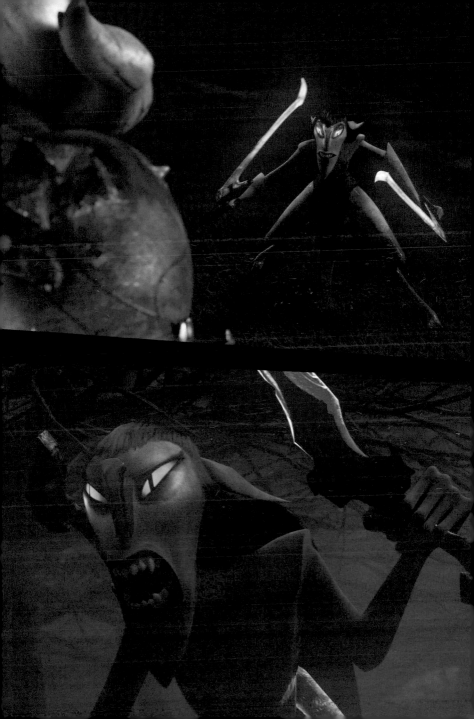

CHAPTER 3
BAPTISM BY FIRE

The Sword of Eclipse slashed through another blazing jet of fire, diverting it into two smaller streams that fizzled into smoke beside him. Jim twirled his blade in the air to cool it, then caught its hilt with his other hand. For a brief moment, Jim was reminded of how he used to do the same trick back home with his kitchen knives. He longed for those days when his biggest problem was poaching the perfect egg—not facing off against talking fireballs. Snapping back to the present, Jim concentrated on the task at hand.

"WHO ARE YOU?" repeated the fireball as it launched another rippling wave of flames.

Jim ducked, rolled, and activated the shield on his gauntlet. Now black and red like the rest of his armor, the shield withstood this new searing volley. Jim felt sweat pouring down his face, but at least he was still alive and not *roasted* alive.

"I'm the Trollhunter," Jim answered. "I'm here to save an innocent baby. Nothing can get in my way. Especially an overgrown firefly like you!"

Once the flames burned out, Jim jumped for cover behind a heavy boulder and concentrated. The scorched shield and sword dissipated from Jim's hands, only to be replaced with the two Glaives. Jim interlocked the pair of blades into a single weapon and hurled it at the fireball. The Glaives spun through the air in a razor-sharp arc, narrowly missing their target.

"YOUR PUNY TRINKETS HAVE NO EFFECT ON ME, INTRUDER!" said the fireball, even as the Glaives circled back toward it like a boomerang. "I AM THE UNENDING FIRE! I AM INFERNO INCARNATE! I AM—"

The Glaives sliced through the fireball, splitting it into two smaller spheres.

"ACK!" said both fireballs before they fell to the ground.

Jim caught the Glaives on their return and separated them. He approached the two downed fireballs, training his Glaives on them. But to Jim's surprise, the fireballs didn't fly again. Instead, they merged back into a single ball, which, in turn, changed shape into a humanlike figure—albeit one covered from head to toe in living flames.

"Looks like this was my last case after all, partner," said the fiery figure. "And with only two weeks left until retirement."

"What?" Jim asked, his eyes bulging as the figure held out a friendly, but flaming, hand.

"Maybe we should start over," said the figure.

"Start over?!" Jim said. "You were just trying to barbeque me!"

"The only way to survive the Darklands is by killing everything else in the Darklands," said the fire-being as he stood up and dusted himself off. "The name's Rob, by the way."

"Rob?" Jim repeated. "I thought you were the Unending Fire or Inferno Incarnate or something?"

"Yeah, sure, but my friends just call me Rob," Rob said with a shrug.

"You . . . have friends?" Jim asked, unable to hide his skepticism.

"I do now!" Rob replied.

"Unbelievable," muttered Jim as started to walk away. "As if the Darklands weren't weird enough . . ."

Rob followed Jim, leaving fiery footprints as he went, and said, "Slow down, partner. Just because I am a machine does not mean I cannot feel love."

Jim stopped and stared at Rob, studying what passed for his face under all those flames.

"I know that line," Jim said. "It's from my best friend's favorite movie, *Gun Robot*."

"*Gun Robot 3*, actually," Rob said with a burning smile.

"So what you said before, about your 'last case before retirement,'" added Jim with dawning understanding.

"*Gun Robot 2*," confirmed Rob. "And the whole 'WHO ARE YOU' bit? That's from the thrilling climax of *Gun Robot*, when Gun Robot learns the true identity of the mad genius who created him— Doctor Despot. Instant classic, man! And the reason I named myself Rob. It's short for *Robot*!"

Jim's mouth hung open for a while before he managed to say, "How do you know about *Gun Robot*?"

"Ah, some careless Changeling dropped a TV, VCR, and videotapes through a Fetch portal back in the 1980s," said Rob. "I must've watched *Gun Robots 1* through *4* thousands of times through the years. Plus the entire Moral Weapons series. Those movies taught me everything—how to speak, how to disarm bombs at the last second, how to take the law into your own hands. . . . I only stopped watching once the tapes burned out!"

"Um . . . ooookay," Jim said.

Jim headed to the labyrinth's entrance, leaving Rob behind. He tried not to think about the dry feeling in his throat. But the Darklands' winds and the heat coming off Rob only worsened Jim's thirst.

The Trollhunter paused at the mouth of the maze. He wasn't sure which direction to go. Jim looked back and forth between two paths before finally taking a step to the right.

"Wouldn't do that, partner," cautioned Rob, who was now standing uncomfortably close to Jim again. "My robot sensors detect danger that way."

"You're not a robot!" Jim said. "You're just an extremely warm, extremely annoying Changeling!"

"ERROR! ERROR!" Rob said in a robotic voice, before returning to his normal one. "I'm a *Heetling*— the missing link between Changelings and Helheetis."

"The fire-cats?" asked Jim. "Those Helheetis?"

"Yup," Rob said, rocking back and forth on his heels. "My dad did say Mom was quite the hottie . . . before she ate him. Anyway, you're looking at their bouncing, burning bundle of joy. And your best chance of navigating the Darklands."

The Trollhunter rolled his eyes and took another step toward the right, before a bloodcurdling shriek sounded from farther down that path.

"You really know your way around here?" Jim asked, his eyes still glued in the direction of whatever made that awful screech.

"Yep, I'll show you around—for a price," said Rob.

Jim gritted his teeth and asked, "Which is?"

"I get you in and out of this maze alive, and you take me back with you the surface so I can finally see *Gun Robot 5, 6,* and *7!*" Rob squealed.

"What about *Gun Robot 8*?" said Jim.

"There's a *Gun Robot 8*?!" Rob exclaimed. "Well, what're we waiting for, Trollhunter? Follow me if you want to live!"

Rob transformed back into a fireball and zoomed down the left path. Jim slapped his hand against his forehead and reluctantly followed his new guide.

CHAPTER 4
PHANTOM PAINS

Far across the Darklands, Gunmar the Black sat atop his skull-shaped throne that had been carved from the husk of a dying Heartstone. The crystal seat poured its energies into Gunmar, making the blue veins across his body pulse brighter.

Kodanth and Dictatious knelt at the base of Gunmar's throne. The flickering energy cast sinister shadows across their faces.

"You're looking more powerful than ever, Dark Underlord," said Kodanth.

"Lies," Gunmar replied as he stood to his full, impressive height. "This Heartstone dies, as does everything in this place. Soon, it won't have enough power left to recharge me."

"Th-that is," Kodanth tried to explain. "What I

actually meant to say was . . ."

Gunmar descended from his throne and brushed past the stammering adviser. Dictatious smiled to himself under his hood as his master stood in the middle of the Crucible Pit. Gunmar grabbed black sand from the arena's stained floor and let it trickle from his claw like some barbaric hourglass.

"This Crucible Pit has been the stronghold that I—the Black, the Vicious, the Skullcrusher—built to show my dominance over the Darklands," Gunmar said with a snarl. "Now it seems as though it's a tomb. Bular came so close to freeing me months ago, before—"

Gunmar was about to say more, but his body suddenly seized as a sharp pain shot through his skull. He clutched at his missing eye while the remaining one flared in agony. Dictatious ran past the stunned Kodanth to Gunmar's side.

"What ails you, great Gunmar?" Dictatious asked.

"My Eye," said Gunmar, recovering. "Though it has been lost for centuries, it felt like it had suddenly returned to its socket."

"Or somewhere very close," Dictatious suggested.

"Could it be?" Gunmar said. "My Eye? Here? In the Darklands?"

"*I* won't lie to you," Dictatious continued, tossing a pointed look at Kodanth. "Your son, Bular, was among the finest of Gumm-Gumm warriors. Yet the human Trollhunter managed to thwart Bular's plan to return you the surface *and* best him in battle."

"Choose your next words carefully," Gunmar threatened, but Dictatious didn't flinch.

"The point being, sire, that if he could defeat one so formidable as Bular, then it's conceivable the Trollhunter might have also obtained your Eye."

"Impossible," Kodanth protested. "What about the Janus Order? My network of Changeling spies has protected the Eye of Gunmar since—"

"And yet our Dark Underlord senses its presence nearby," Dictatious interrupted. "Surely you don't doubt he who tamed the Darklands . . . do you, Kodanth?"

Now Gunmar fixed his stare upon Kodanth, who shrank under the severe gaze.

"N-no, of course not," replied a trembling Kodanth.

"And if the Trollhunter followed the Last Rites

of Bodus to collect your Birthstone, Killstone, and Eye . . . ," Dictatious began.

"Then the fool has now come here in a pathetic attempt to stop me," said Gunmar in understanding. "And, more importantly, has left a portal back to the surface lands. One which I can force him to open. . . ."

"Your brilliance never ceases to astound, my Dark Underlord. The way you pieced all that together—clearly you have no need for an adviser such as I. Let alone *two* . . . ," Dictatious said with a smirk aimed at Kodanth.

Gunmar's eye flickered as he thought over Dictatious's words. Finally, he spoke.

"Dictatious, dispatch my deadliest soldiers to scour the Darklands in search of Merlin's champion. If the Trollhunter who robbed me of my son has crossed into this accursed dimension, I would have words with him . . . right before I feast on his entrails and wipe the gore from my jaws with a rag made of his skin."

"I will escort them personally, Master," Dictatious said with a bow.

"And what of your loyal servant, Kodanth?" asked the orange Changeling. "Sh-shall I—"

"You shall investigate your Janus Order," commanded Gunmar. "And discover how they allowed my Eye to fall into the Trollhunter's possession under your so-called . . . *leadership*."

Gunmar lumbered past his two advisers—one pleased, one terrified—and stood before a large gate composed of crystalline orange spikes. He grunted, and the crystal shards retreated into the bedrock, revealing a deep cavern.

"Both of you, leave me to my Horde," Gunmar ordered. "I must ready them to hunt my other nemesis, Skarlagk. Her rebellion has been a light-ray in my side for far too long. How fitting, then, that *both* of my enemies shall soon meet the same bloody fate."

Gunmar descended into the cavern, and the spikes stabbed out again to close the passage behind him. A moment later, a loud chorus of monstrous animal sounds echoed from within the cavern as Gunmar greeted his Horde. Kodanth shuddered at the horrific noise, but Dictatious didn't seem disturbed in the slightest.

"I think that went well," he said cheerfully before patting Kodanth on the back with four hands and strolling out of the Crucible Pit.

CHAPTER 5
SEEING DOUBLE

Draal the Deadly prowled through Arcadia Oaks's dense woods, moving surprisingly silently for such a big Troll. He was careful to stick to the shadows, avoiding the sun—and any unwanted attention from the humans. They would likely scream at the sight of his spiked body. Draal's coppery mechanical arm parted the bushes in front of him, revealing Barbara just ahead.

Barbara wandered in a daze down the sidewalk that ran alongside the tree line. She was dressed in her usual doctor's uniform of green scrubs and sneakers. But Barbara seemed lost, even though she was in her own neighborhood, and her eyes appeared unfocused behind her glasses.

Draal's nostrils twitched as he sensed a subtle

shift in the air around him. A split second later, a shadow opened beside him, depositing Claire, Toby, and NotEnrique into the woods.

"I see you received my message concerning Ba-Bru-Ah," Draal whispered.

"That ain't how ya say her name, ya glork," NotEnrique hissed. "It's spelled Barbara. B-A-R-B—"

"Save the vocab lesson for later," Claire said as she hushed them. "Draal, we came as soon as we could. Good thing you make a solid emotional anchor for my Shadow Staff. Now, what happened?"

Draal whispered, "I hid in the shady tree outside of the ha-spoo-tahl—"

"That's *hospital*," NotEnrique corrected.

Draal sneered at the green imp and continued. "I kept my oath to guard the Trollhunter's mother. Only she seems to have healed from her spell earlier than expected. No doubt due to the interference of your ridiculous human medicines!"

"Oh no!" Claire exclaimed, pointing at Barbara. "She just turned onto her street!"

"Let's move!" said Toby as he bolted out of the woods and onto the sidewalk.

Claire followed with NotEnrique in her arms and

watched the Changeling transform into a beautiful blond baby. Now the spitting image of the *real* Enrique, he blew a raspberry at Draal and said, "Too bad you can't follow us into the sunlight, Draal the *Dopey*!"

"*Impure* scoundrel," Draal murmured as the others caught up with Barbara.

"Doctor Lake!" Claire called out.

Barbara turned around and saw Toby, Claire, and what appeared to be her baby brother running toward her.

"Toby! Claire!" Barbara said with a shaky voice. "Shouldn't you be in school with Jim?"

"Our school's, um, closed," Toby fibbed. "Due to an outbreak of, uh, head lice!"

"And it, er, spread to Enrique's day care too!" Claire added.

NotEnrique pretended to scratch an itch in his blond hair, completing the lie.

"Oh," said Barbara, swaying on her feet.

"You okay there, Doctor L?" Toby asked. "No offense, but you seem kinda wobbly."

"Just recovering from a concussion," Barbara said with a weak laugh. "Apparently, Jim drove me to the hospital yesterday after I accidentally slipped and hit my head at home."

Barbara paused. Her brow creased, as if she was trying to recall something just at the edge of her memory.

"At least, I *think* that's what Jim told me," she added. "He couldn't stay long. Jim said he had to do something . . . something important. Where is Jim anyway? I couldn't find my car at the hospital, and he hasn't been answering any of my calls."

She continued down the sidewalk, and Claire and Toby exchanged a nervous look. They ran in front of her again, trying to block Barbara's path.

"Who, Jim? Jim Lake Junior? Your son?" Toby rambled, stalling for time. "He's, uh, back at school."

"But I thought you said school was closed?" Barbara asked.

"I mean he's at, ah, culinary school!" Toby said. "Didn't he tell you he's taking cooking lessons on the side? That scamp!"

"Really?" said Barbara, confused. "My son should be *teaching* cooking lessons."

"I know, right?" Claire took over, now standing

directly in front of Barbara. "But you know Jim. So dedicated to his craft."

"I . . . guess . . . ," Barbara said as she side-stepped Claire and continued on her way.

"We gotta do something!" said Toby in an urgent whisper. "We're less than a block from *casa del Jimbo*!"

NotEnrique gave the A-OK sign and said, "Time to dust off me best material."

The baby in Claire's arms started to cry at the top of his lungs. Barbara paused at the corner of her street and looked back at "Enrique."

"What's the matter, little guy?" Barbara said in a soothing, motherly voice.

NotEnrique winked at Claire and Toby before wailing louder than ever.

"Let Doctor Lake have a look-see," said Barbara as she took the baby into her arms. "Oh, yes, Jim used to cry like this when he was hungry. How about we get you back to your home and find you a nice, warm bottle?"

Toby and Claire privately fist-bumped as Barbara started leading them away from her block. They managed to go a few feet before a police car sped past them, its sirens blaring as it made a sharp turn down Barbara's street.

"What in the world . . . ," she wondered aloud. "Hang tight, guys. Someone might be hurt."

Barbara handed Enrique back to Claire and broke into a run after the police car. Toby and Claire turned to NotEnrique in surprise.

"Don't blame me," he said. "The ol' waterworks always kill with the lady types!"

The trio took off after Barbara and found her standing in front of her driveway. Only she wasn't alone. The front lawn was completely overrun with police activity. Several black-and-white squad cars sat parked outside, lights spinning. Uniformed cops strung yellow POLICE LINE DO NOT CROSS tape around the yard. And beyond them, Barbara's house stood in shambles, its front door kicked open and tons of interior damage visible through the windows.

"Jim!" cried Barbara as she rushed up to the police. "My son—is he in there?"

Detective Scott of the Arcadia Oaks Police Department met Barbara at the edge of her property, his hands held up in a calming gesture.

"Easy, Doctor Lake," said Detective Scott.

"Nobody's hurt, thank goodness. Neighbors reported strange sounds coming from your place last night and then saw the mess this morning. Looks like your home was broken into while you were gone. Fortunately, nothing appears to be missing. Except your car, that is."

Barbara massaged the sides of her head, trying to stay calm and recall recent events.

"It isn't missing," Barbara finally replied. "Jim drove me to the hospital. He must still have it."

"Nah, your car's totaled," Toby blurted out, before immediately covering his big mouth with his hands. At least he left out the part about Barbara's car getting wrecked in an epic battle for Heartstone Trollmarket.

"He means *totally*, uh, clean!" Claire improvised unconvincingly. "Because Jim, um, took it to the car wash? While he's still in culinary school? Due to the aforementioned head-lice situation at our school?"

Barbara and Detective Scott both stared at Claire and Toby in utter disbelief.

"Tobias Domzalski and Claire Nuñez, I'm starting to think neither of you are being completely honest with me," Barbara said sternly.

"No, we, uh," Toby blathered. "I mean, he—she—I—it's, it's—"

"It's okay!" came a familiar voice from behind them.

Everyone turned and discovered the last person they expected to see.

"I can explain everything," said Jim Lake Jr. from under the shade of a tall oak tree. "Rest assured, this situation is totally under control!"

CHAPTER 6
LABYRINTHINE AND SERPENTINE

"This situation is totally out of control!" said Jim.

"Whattaya mean, *amigo*?" said Rob as he darted along the labyrinth, lighting their way with his body, like a torch.

Every time he landed at a new spot in the maze, Rob left behind a small patch of fire, which Jim had to stomp out with his armored feet.

"It's Doctor Despot, isn't it?" Rob went on. "Don't worry. We're gonna blow his entire crime syndicate sky-high, rescue the mayor, and still get you home in time for your daughter's piano recital. So swears Gun—"

"You're not Gun Robot!" yelled Jim. "I'm not Gun Robot's partner! And there is no Doctor Despot! We're in the Darklands—not the plot of *Gun Robot 2*!"

"*Gun Robot 3*, you mean," Rob corrected. "But you're right. I should just learn to be myself around friends."

"We're not friends!" Jim scowled as he stamped out another blaze.

"Oh, okay," said Rob, his fiery lips pouting. "I get it. I mean, who'd want to be friends with a burning freak like me?"

Jim sighed despite himself. Seeing Rob standing there with his head stooped and his lit arms hanging at his sides, Jim couldn't help but feel sympathy for him.

"I . . . I'm sorry, Rob," said Jim. "It's got nothing to do with you. I . . . I'm just keeping a strict 'no friends' policy while I'm down here. I need my mind clear of all emotional attachments so I can do whatever it takes to rescue Enrique and stop Gunmar."

"Aw, I could never stay mad at you!" Rob said, instantly happy again. "Now, let's high-five, freeze-frame, and roll credits!"

Jim let out an irritated groan and marched past Rob's outstretched hand. The Trollhunter continued along their chosen path until he reached yet another fork in the road.

"Wait," said Jim as he studied his surroundings. "Weren't we at this exact same spot *hours* ago?"

"Huh, I dunno. All these passageways start looking the same after a while," Rob said as he rubbed his chin in thought.

"Didn't you say you could lead me through this maze?" Jim asked, his anger rising.

"Sure," Rob said. "Eventually."

"Eventually?!" Jim hollered.

His loud voice echoed throughout the labyrinth, until another dreadful shriek answered it.

"That . . . sounded close," Jim said in a voice that had grown hoarse with thirst.

"Lock and load," Rob replied as he made finger guns with his fire hands.

Jim concentrated once again, and the Sword of Eclipse and Shield returned in a black-and-red flash. The Trollhunter held a *shh* finger to his chapped lips as he crept past Rob and up to the fork in the road. Taking a deep breath, Jim slowly craned his head down the left tunnel. Empty. Jim's body unclenched. Steadying his nerves, he then approached the right tunnel and peeked into it.

A gargantuan, glowing eel sprang out of the

darkness and snapped at the Trollhunter with rows upon rows of spiny teeth.

"Whoa!" shouted Jim before he stumbled backward, narrowly avoiding the bite.

The bioluminescent serpent screeched again in hunger and slithered out of the tunnel, blocking both sides of the fork with its long, coiled body.

"Nyarlagroth!" cried Rob as the eel circled them. "Run for it!"

Rob shot flames at the Nyarlagroth, all while making sound effects with his mouth. But the flames didn't affect the eel in the slightest. Its radiant, leathery skin didn't even have a singe mark on it.

"Oh right," Rob remembered. "These guys are fireproof."

The Nyarlagroth released its most deafening shriek yet. Jim covered his ears and ran, with Rob hot on his heels. They retraced their steps, turning left, right, right again, then left—no, right—no, left!—until Jim's armored body slammed into a dead end.

His head still ringing from the impact and the Nyarlagroth's screech, Jim pushed himself off the cold stone floor and looked around. The Trollhunter discovered he was all alone.

"Rob?" Jim called out. "Where are you?"

A faint glow appeared just beyond the dead end, and Jim chuckled in relief.

"Whew!" Jim said as the glow grew closer and brighter. "I thought we got separated back there, Rob. You gave me quite a—"

Jim's next word caught in his throat as the source of the glow reached the dead end.

"—scare."

Jim swallowed hard as the Nyarlagroth, not Rob, cornered him. Its lips peeled back, exposing teeth as tall as Jim, if not taller. The eel's jaws parted, and a long tongue lanced out. It wrapped around the Trollhunter like a tentacle. Jim heard the plates of his armor crunch and scrape as the tongue started to squeeze.

"Gah!" Jim wheezed, the air being forced from his lungs.

He tried to summon the Glaives to appear in his hands, but Jim found it harder and harder to concentrate. He began to black out. With his vision growing murky, Jim could only watch helplessly as the Nyarlagroth pulled him closer to its open, dripping mouth. The Trollhunter shut his eyes, bracing for the worst, until another shrill cry filled the dead end.

Jim felt the tongue suddenly loosen around his body before it dropped him to the cold ground again. Gasping for air, Jim struggled to his feet and looked up with blurry eyes.

The Nyarlagroth lay motionless before him, its tongue lolling on the floor and a huge rusted spear jutting from its side. A female Gumm-Gumm with powerfully muscular arms emerged from the darkness and retrieved her spear from the Nyarlagroth.

"I am Skarlagk the Scorned, daughter of Orlagk," she said. "And I have an offer for you, Trollhunter: join me so that we might take up arms against Gunmar together."

Jim's eyes went wide with surprise before they rolled back in his head. The Sword of Eclipse vanished, the armor's red lines faded, and the Trollhunter—still reeling from a lack of oxygen—fainted fast at Skarlagk's feet.

CHAPTER 7
SWITCHEROO

"And so, as you can see, this was all just a rather large misunderstanding," Jim continued from under the shady tree in front of his home. "While Barbara—that is to say, my mother—recuperated in the hospital following her concussion, I foolishly hosted a party at our house. A little pre-Spring Fling bash for my fellow students, if you will."

"A . . . bash?" asked Barbara and Detective Scott simultaneously.

Toby, Claire, and NotEnrique seemed just as confused as the grown-ups and policemen who had gathered around Jim.

"Alas, yes," Jim said. "But this turned out to be an unfortunate lapse in judgment on my part, as the festivities soon grew out of hand. Too many guests tried to fit inside, some furniture broke, and, well, we trashed the place. I take full responsibility for my actions and apologize for any inconvenience to you fine, upstanding law enforcement officials."

Jim beamed an unnaturally wide smile at his mom, who stared back at him. In fact, everyone was staring a Jim. Even Draal, who watched dumbfounded from some nearby bushes.

"Teenagers," grumbled Detective Scott as he folded up his notebook. "False alarm, guys. Let's pack it up."

As the police left grumbling, Jim turned to the stunned Toby and Claire and gave them a knowing wink.

As the sun set, Claire, Toby, and NotEnrique—back in his Changeling form—watched through Jim's bedroom window as the last police car pulled out of the driveway.

"That . . . was close," said Claire.

"No kidding," NotEnrique agreed. "I think I almost soiled meself."

"Me too," Toby said just as the bedroom door opened behind them.

Jim entered quietly and whispered, "I finally got Barbara to take a nap. By the time she wakes, the last effects of the memory spell will have worn off. Even today's excitement with the police will seem like a distant dream and—"

His last words became muffled as Toby and Claire rushed up and embraced Jim. Even NotEnrique got in on the group hug, until he realized what he was doing and let go of Jim's leg.

"Jim! I've been wanting to do this the second I saw you!" Claire said, her voice thick with emotion.

"How'd you get back, Jimbo?" asked Toby, his arms still wrapped around his best friend. "And just how hard did you kick Gunmar's Gumm-Gumm butt?!"

Jim looked down in disappointment. Toby and Claire released him and took a step back.

"Jim?" Claire said. "What is it? Are you okay?"

"No, actually," Jim began. "In point of fact, I'm not even me."

With a heavy sigh, Jim reached behind his head and pulled off his own face. Blinky now stood where Jim had a moment ago, holding a bizarre tiki-like mask in two of his four hands. Claire gasped.

"Blinky?!" Toby exclaimed. "That was you this whole time?"

"I'm afraid so, Tobias," said Blinky. "I apologize for the deception. I merely wanted to help all of you—and Barbara—in Jim's absence. This Glamour Mask seemed like the best way to do so . . . at the time."

NotEnrique's round yellow eyes looked from the mask to Claire. She pursed her lips tightly, as if she wanted to say something, but was holding back.

"Hey, sponge-face," NotEnrique said in an unusually soft manner. "What's the matter?"

"It's nothing," Claire said quickly, turning her back to them and wiping something from her eye.

"And you were right about that Glamour Mask, Blinky," Claire continued, now back to business. "It'll definitely help cover for Jim at school and home. At least until he comes back."

"Yeah, but maybe Claire or I should be the ones to wear it," Toby said.

He carefully took the mask from Blinky's hands and examined the bizarre patterns etched into its surface. "No offense, but you use way more SAT words than the average human!"

"Indubitably!" said Blinky proudly.

"Where'd you even *find* this thing?" Toby asked, turning the mask in his hands.

"Ah, now that is a story worth telling," Blinky said with his usual flair. "You see, once you all shadow-jumped away, I scoured my library for a cure to AAARRRGGHH!!!'s concrete condition. During my research, I stumbled upon a reference to the Glamour Mask in *A Brief Recapitulation of Troll Lore*, volume thirty-seven, I think. Or was that volume thirty-eight? No—volume thirty-seven!"

"Cut to the chase, Galadrigal!" NotEnrique barked.

"But of course," Blinky resumed. "As it turns out, Glamour Masks are exceedingly rare artifacts crafted by a Troll civilization that no longer exists. I raced to RotGut's Apothecary and, by Deya's grace, they just happened to have the last known mask in existence. The very mask you now hold in your tender young hands, Master Tobias."

"Finally! Some good luck for a change!" cheered Toby—right before the mask slipped out of his fingers and shattered against the floor into hundreds of tiny pieces.

"Oh, Grumbly Gruesome!" hollered Blinky.

"Um, my bad?" Toby winced in apology.

NotEnrique literally rolled on the floor and laughed out loud. Ignoring him, Claire knelt down beside the mask fragments and tried to fit them back together like puzzle pieces.

"I don't think there's enough super glue in Arcadia Oaks and Trollmarket combined to fix this," she said. "Anyone got a plan—let's see, what letter are we up to by now?"

"Q," grumbled Draal as he climbed through the open window, dusk visible behind him.

"Thanks," said Claire. "Anyone got a Plan Q we can use?"

"No," said Blinky, thoughtfully tapping a finger to his lips. "But I may have a Plan K. . . ."

CHAPTER 8
WHISTLE IN THE DARK

A purple hand reached up to the withered vine and plucked the fruit that sagged from it.

"Mmm, Cimmerian fruit. Smells like . . . death," said Nomura before she took a ravenous bite and snatched some more from the vines.

Nomura couldn't remember the last time she had eaten. The Changeling had grown used to hunger and other discomforts in the months since she'd become trapped in the Darklands. Every time she thought of the reason why—a failed attempt to return Gunmar to the surface that backfired and brought Nomura here—she simmered with rage. But then Nomura would calm herself by whistling her favorite human melody, *Peer Gynt*.

Devouring the rest of the rotted fruit, plus a

few more, Nomura whistled a few bars, before drifting into a long overdue sleep. Yet the muted sounds of nearby movement made her cat eyes snap back open. Nomura sprang to her feet and unsheathed the two scimitars strapped to her back. She scanned the darkness and saw several pairs of beady red eyes glowing back at her.

"Cha-hoon! Cha-hoon!" wailed dozens of tiny voices before a pack of Albino Goblins leaped out at Nomura from behind the wilted vines.

She slapped away a few of the white-skinned, red-eyed creatures with her curved blades and ran from the twisted vineyard. The Goblins chased her like deranged bloodhounds and kept calling, "Cha-hoon! Cha-hoon!"

With her long, muscular legs, Nomura easily outpaced the Goblin pack. But she halted in the middle of a narrow rope bridge that stretched over a deep pit. Dictatious and a platoon of Gumm-Gumms waited at the other end, their barbed weapons drawn.

"Well, isn't this a surprise?" Dictatious said with menace. "An unregistered Changeling running free in the Darklands."

Nomura looked back and saw the Goblins massing at the other end. Trapped, she peered over the side of the rope bridge and saw nothing but endless black beneath her.

"Did you enter our realm with the Trollhunter?" Dictatious asked. "The human they call Jim Lake Junior?"

A bitter laugh overcame Nomura. The Goblins and Gumm-Gumms all looked at one another, not getting the joke.

"The Trollhunter?" she cackled. "You'd find him in *pieces* if we'd traveled together."

Dictatious arched his six eyebrows and said, "Charming, I'm sure. But tell me, if not the Trollhunter, then what, exactly, brings you to the domain of Gunmar the Vicious?"

"As if I'd tell a scheming underling like you." Nomura smirked.

She took a step backward and almost lost her footing. A few pebbles dropped off the rope bridge and disappeared in the darkness below. Nomura regained her balance, but remained slightly distracted since she never heard those pebbles hit the bottom.

"It doesn't look like you have much choice," Dictatious said, and then sneered before addressing the Gumm-Gumm soldiers. "Make it painful."

Dictatious's cloak swirled as he turned on his heels and walked away from the bridge. The Gumm-Gumms and Goblins closed in on Nomura, bloodlust in their manic eyes. She gripped her scimitars tighter.

"You still have one last chance to save your life," Nomura called out.

Dictatious looked back at her with bemused curiosity and asked, "Save *my* life?"

"That's right," Nomura answered. "All who serve Gunmar know of his distaste for failure. I've trekked from one end of the Darklands to the other just to avoid his vengeance."

"The only failure my six eyes see here is you, *Impure*," Dictatious spat.

His four arms flashed a signal, and the Gumm-Gumms and Goblins encroached upon Nomura once again. But rather than strike out at her enemies, Nomura relaxed and returned her swords to the scabbards on her back.

"True," she said. "But if I die, I take the location

of Skarlagk's hidden fortress with me."

Dictatious's six eyes went wide. Nomura smirked again.

"Wait!" Dictatious ordered, and everyone froze. "You know, a long time ago, I also bartered for my life in the Darklands. I betrayed others—Trolls I admired, even respected—so that I might survive. You'd do the same, Changeling?"

"That's right," said Nomura. "I've been here long enough to know Gunmar hates Skarlagk almost as much as he does the Trollhunter. And only *I* know where to find her. But if you end me before I can share that information with Gunmar . . . well, who's the *failure* now?"

Nomura laughed again. Dictatious considered the offer. And those pebbles finally hit the bottom.

CHAPTER 9
UNDERGROUND RESISTANCE

Much to his surprise, the Trollhunter woke up alive.

Jim winced. His ribs were still sore from earlier. His tongue felt like sandpaper inside of his dry, sticky mouth. His skull throbbed with a splitting head- ache. And now he found himself on top of another Nyarlagroth as it moved through the Darklands. Reacting on instinct, Jim jumped to his feet. The Sword of Eclipse returned to his armored hand in a whirl of mist and magic.

"You'll find this Nyarlagroth a little tamer than the last," said a husky voice.

Jim spun around and found Skarlagk standing at the head of the enormous eel, controlling its motions with the chains in her hands. Approaching carefully, Jim looked over Skarlagk's shoulder and saw how her reins connected to a bridle in the Nyarlagroth's jaws. She pulled left, and with another splitting screech, so did the Nyarlagroth.

More screeches resounded behind Jim. Looking back, he saw three more domesticated Nyarlagroths obey their Gumm-Gumm riders.

"No offense, but I didn't take you for the animal-loving type," Jim said. "Seeing as how you speared that other Nyarlagroth and all."

"Would you prefer that I had speared you instead?" Skarlagk asked flatly. "Put you out of your misery before the Nyarlagroth devoured you?"

Jim thought it over and said, "Fair point. Thank you . . . Skarlagk, is it?"

She nodded, the spears in her quiver clattering together as the Nyarlagroth carried them over a particularly rugged stretch of wasteland. Jim raised his eyebrows, impressed by how much ground they were covering in such a short time.

"I guess Nyarlagroths are the *only* way to travel in the Darklands, huh?" he joked feebly.

"My rebels and I choose to survive alongside the creatures native to this dark dimension, unlike Gunmar. He would crush them under his heel without a second thought," Skarlagk answered.

"Yeah, about Gunmar," Jim resumed. "I seem to recall you mentioning something about us teaming up against him. Before I, y'know, passed out."

Skarlagk looked upon Jim with eyes as dark as storm clouds, then nodded again. Jim pointed his sword at the three Gumm-Gumms who piloted the Nyarlagroths in formation behind them.

"Well, not that I don't appreciate the extra help," Jim continued. "But I don't see how a handful of rebels on overgrown earthworms necessarily improves our chances. Especially against a guy who uses the word 'Skullcrusher' in his job description!"

"A handful won't help you against Gunmar," said Skarlagk as she pulled back on her reins, halting the Nyarlagroth on top of a high ridge. "But an army might."

Jim's jaw hung open as he took in the sight of the blighted valley below them. There, a titanic stone fortress teemed with hundreds upon hundreds of rebel Gumm-Gumms. They ran drills along its battlements and practiced close combat in the open ward at the center. A bulky obsidian roof covered the ramparts, the black volcanic glass glinting in the endless twilight, while thick fog obscured the castle's foundation. From the highest tower, a billowing flag bore an image of Gunmar's eye with a red slash painted across it.

Jim stood in awe before a fully armed fighting force. From her Nyarlagroth steed, Skarlagk held a spear high in the air. The rebels on the fortress returned the salute, chanting, "SKARLAGK! SKARLAGK! SKARLAGK!"

Once the Nyarlagroths had been stabled, Skarlagk led Jim inside her stronghold. He stared agog at the fearsome rebels who looked back from the parapets. Most of the Gumm-Gumms cursed under their breath at the sight of the Trollhunter. Some even spat at his armor.

"Your soldiers remind me a lot of this guy I know, Steve," said Jim as he dodged the phlegmy spitballs and stuck close to Skarlagk. "He likes to bully people too."

"Pay them no mind," Skarlagk said. "Some still harbor ill will against one of your predecessors, Deya. But even that grudge pales in comparison to the one they hold for Gunmar."

Jim stepped over a heaping pile of dung—he

WELCOME TO THE DARKLANDS

didn't want to guess *what* had left it—and said, "And here I thought all Gumm-Gumms worshipped him."

"Not all . . . ," answered Skarlagk.

Her face tightened momentarily before returning to its usual impassive state. This was the first hint of emotion Skarlagk had shown since Jim met her. Recovering, she pointed her spear at the soldiers around them. Every one of them knelt before their warrior queen's presence.

"And these ones broke from Gunmar after our defeat at the Battle of Killahead," Skarlagk said. "Many still blame him for losing to Deya and, thus, for our exile to the Darklands. When I started this rebellion to seek retribution against Gunmar, they were only too eager to enlist."

Reaching the heart of the keep, Skarlagk threw open the doors to the mess hall, where dozens of Gumm-Gumm rebels gathered. She indicated a spot for Jim in the middle of a long battered bench, while she took her seat at the head of an equally long, equally battered table.

Jim squeezed between two oversized rebels who must have each been quadruple his size. His eyes searched the hall for food but found none. The mess hall doors kicked open again, and more Gumm-Gumms entered carrying deep stone bowls. Half the bowls held boiling water, while the others overflowed with what looked to be round red rocks.

Jim elbowed the Gumm-Gumm beside him and whispered, "What're those?"

The rebel looked down at him in astonishment and asked, "You've never seen a Nyarlagroth egg before, fleshbag?"

Hungry enough to eat pretty much anything, Jim grabbed an egg and prepared to crack it. The same rebel slapped him on the back of the head, motioning toward one of the bowls with water.

"Ya gotta boil the egg first," said the Gumm-Gumm. "Eat it raw, and ya might as well chug a flagon of Gnome poison!"

The nearby rebels all laughed heartily at Jim, but he ignored them. Jim stared at the scalding water and licked his parched lips. He was so thirsty, Jim considered dunking his entire head in the bowl before deciding against it. Placing the egg on the end of his Sword of Eclipse, the Trollhunter lowered it into the steaming water, just like the Gumm-Gumms around him.

"Looks like I get to practice my poaching skills in the Darklands, after all," Jim said and smiled.

When they retrieved their eggs, Jim did the same, juggling the egg in his hands. After it was cool enough, Jim cracked open the shell and nearly gagged at the sight and smell of a runny, rancid yolk.

He looked around and watched, aghast, as the Gumm-Gumms downed their eggs in a single slurp each. None of them seemed to keel over . . . yet. Despite his better judgment, Jim closed his eyes, said a quiet prayer, and poured the slimy egg into his mouth.

It was like swallowing warm liquid garbage. Jim immediately coughed it out, and the entire mess hall erupted in Gumm-Gumm laughter. The only one who didn't laugh was Skarlagk.

"Guess that's an acquired taste," Jim said, still spitting up gummy bits of yolk. "But it beats Chicken Surprise."

Queasy, Jim looked to the head of the table, but found Skarlagk gone. Jim stood, clearly unable to choke down anymore soft-boiled swill for the time being. He left the others laughing behind him and walked out of the mess hall in search of their sullen leader.

As he wandered the fortress, Jim came to a grim realization. He had no idea where he was, how long he'd been unconscious on the Nyarlagroth, or which way he had to go to find Enrique. Jim hadn't felt this lost since he was in that labyrinth with . . .

"Rob," Jim murmured to himself, only now remembering his *guide*.

He didn't know where the obnoxious spitfire had gone and, frankly, Jim didn't care.

No friends in the Darklands, Jim mentally reminded himself of his policy.

Rounding a corner, the Trollhunter finally found Skarlagk in what must have been her chambers. The place seemed more like a war room, with a sprawling map of the Darklands sketched in white chalk across the full length of the slate walls. Skarlagk drew a few more details in one of the corners. Once finished, she dropped the nub of chalk into her satchel. She then stared intently at this new portion of the map, as if trying to memorize it.

"I use chalk so I can erase it at a moment's

notice," Skarlagk said before Jim could ask. "We've always managed to stay one step ahead of Gunmar's forces. But the moment we let down our guard is surely the very moment he will strike."

"Surely," Jim agreed. "But Gunmar's been here as long as you, right? He's gotta have a map of all the places he's been to in the Darklands."

"This shows more than where we've been," Skarlagk said. "It shows where we're going."

She stomped her boot powerfully against the stone floor one time, and the whole fortress rumbled. Jim steadied himself by the war room's open window and yelled, "What is that?!"

Skarlagk joined Jim at the portico and pointed at the dense shroud of fog below them. A colossal Nyarlagroth—at least fifty times larger than any Jim had seen—rose from the haze, lifting the entirety of Skarlagk's fortress, which had been built upon its back.

"A Nyarlagroth queen," said Skarlagk. "*That* is how we stay one step ahead of Gunmar. She moves us to one of nine secure locations across the Darklands every few days."

"Unbelievable," Jim said, boggled by the incredible

scale of the beast beneath them. "But . . . *why*? Why all this for Gunmar? I mean, yeah, I kinda get it. After all, he's promised to make 'an ocean of blood from my loved ones.' And . . . and 'a throne from their bones.' But to devote your entire existence to getting even with one enemy? To be on the run from him for centuries? That's just, well . . . crazy."

Skarlagk did not speak. Instead, she reached into her satchel, pulled out the old horned skull, and pressed it lovingly against her forehead.

"This belonged to my father, Orlagk," Skarlagk said, her voice barely above a whisper. "Until Gunmar betrayed him."

Jim's eyes softened in understanding. He wanted to reach out, to say something to her. But he didn't know what.

"He did this in front of me, as I hid like a coward in the shadows. Then he assumed control of my father's Gumm-Gumm army," she continued.

"How . . . how old were you?" Jim finally said.

"Almost sixteen, in your human years," Skarlagk answered.

"Skarlagk, you weren't a coward," Jim said. "You were a *teenager*."

"Explain that to my father," said Skarlagk as she put away the skull. "Ever since that moment, I have dedicated myself to demolishing Gunmar and everything for which he stands. Now that I've found you, I finally have the weapon I need to fulfill my life's mission and avenge my father."

The Trollhunter remained quiet, trying to process all that he had heard. Although Skarlagk had no way of knowing, Jim had just turned sixteen himself. The very idea of Skarlagk witnessing what she had seen at that age made Jim wonder what he'd do in her situation. All of a sudden, he didn't crave water or a hot shower anymore. It was hard for Jim to feel anything other than a cold emptiness in his chest.

"You have not responded to my offer, Trollhunter," said Skarlagk. "Will you join me? Will you help end Gunmar's reign before he fulfills his promise and does to your loved ones what he did to mine?"

Jim looked up at Skarlagk, his blue eyes meeting her cold, flinty ones. That hollow feeling spread inside of him.

"Yes," said the Trollhunter, unsure of what steep cost it would take on his own soul.

CHAPTER 10
DEAL WITH THE DEVIL

After a long march, the Gumm-Gumm search party shoved a shackled Nomura into the Crucible Pit. Dictatious approached the throne and bowed to Gunmar.

"Dark Underlord, we have yet to find any evidence of the Trollhunter's presence in the Darklands," Dictatious began. "But this rogue *Impure* we discovered may bring you some small measure of satisfaction."

Gunmar stood, and Nomura's defiant posture faltered. But she quickly recovered and stared back into his lone, livid eye.

"I recognize you," Gunmar said, his stinking breath hitting Nomura like a fist.

Kodanth scrambled into the Crucible Pit, late to

the scene. He glanced at Dictatious, who wagged four disapproving fingers—one on each hand—at Kodanth.

"Tell me, Kodanth, does she seem familiar to you, as well?" Gunmar went on.

"Y-yes, Master," stammered Kodanth, relieved that Gunmar hadn't mentioned his tardiness. "Nomura is a member of my Janus Order."

"Is that so?" Gunmar asked, still not taking his eye off Nomura. "I, too, remember her. As one of the Changelings who failed me when Bular last tried to return me to the surface lands. You do know the price of failure, do you not?"

Gunmar flexed his right claw, and strands of energy weaved the Decimaar Blade into his grasp. Dictatious tried get Gunmar's attention, to stay Nomura's execution. But she beat him to it.

Nomura bent at the knees and flipped high into the air. On her descent, Nomura tucked in her legs, pulled her cuffed arms in front of her body, and landed gracefully. The Gumm-Gumms immediately slashed at her with their axes. But Nomura held out her manacles so that their weapons split the chains that bound her instead. Now freed, she grabbed the scimitars from her scabbards and fought back. Her curved blades struck against the Gumm-Gumms' rusty weapons, setting off showers of sparks that lit up the Crucible Pit.

After clearing a wide circle in the arena, Nomura held out her left sword to keep her attackers at bay. With her right, she traced a fast map into the black sand floor, marking nine distinct spots with large *X*s.

"These are the locations where Skarlagk's fortress crawls every few days," Nomura finally said. "I have tracked them since I first arrived in the Darklands, and only I know their timing and pattern."

Gunmar glared at Nomura, the Decimaar Blade still held firmly in his grasp. Behind him, Dictatious and Kodanth traded an uncertain look.

"Let me live, Gunmar, and I will share these with you," Nomura offered. "If not, well . . ."

Nomura swept away the map with her sword, erasing the *X*s. Gunmar just stood there breathing for quite some time before he said, "Come, Nomura. Whisper what you know into my ear so that you may live and serve Gunmar once again."

Nomura hesitated, her eyes flicking toward

WELCOME TO THE DARKLANDS

Dictatious. But he just held up all his hands in uncertainty. Realizing she didn't have much of a choice, Nomura sheathed her scimitars, walked over to Gunmar, and whispered. She had to stand on the tips of her toes just to reach his ear, even as he hunched over. When she was done, Gunmar nodded and said, "You have kept your end of the bargain. So shall I."

Gunmar cast his eye toward the Gumm-Gumms, and they seized Nomura.

"What's the meaning of this?!" Nomura shouted. "You said that I would live! That I would still serve you!"

She struggled against the Gumm-Gumms, but they ultimately overpowered her.

"You do live," Gunmar answered with an ugly grin. "And you shall serve—a lifetime imprisoned in my dungeons."

"Curse you, Gunmar!" Nomura spat in rage. "Curse you!"

"I already am," Gunmar replied.

The Gumm-Gumms dragged Nomura, twisting and kicking, into a tunnel. More of those orange spikes slid into place behind them like the bars of a crystal prison.

"Lord Gunmar," Kodanth began after Nomura's

anguished cries finally faded. "Surely you've con-sidered that Nomura's information might just be a trap set by Skarlagk herself?"

"I have," said Gunmar. "For I have already suf-fered the folly of trusting a Changeling."

Dictatious watched with glee as Gunmar took a lumbering step toward Kodanth, the Decimaar Blade alight. Under his cloak, Dictatious silently clapped his four hands together.

"W-what?" Kodanth groveled. "You couldn't pos-sibly mean—"

"Such an unpredictable lot," Gunmar continued, taking another step. "Tell me, Kodanth, have you discovered who let my Eye fall into the Trollhunter's hands?"

Kodanth swallowed hard and said, "It could only have been Strickler, sire. He was entrusted with safe-guarding the Eye until your triumphant return to—"

"Ah, another Changeling, then," said Gunmar as he brandished his Decimaar Blade.

"Yes! I mean, no!" Kodanth fumbled. "I mean, I think he sought to use it as a bargaining chip. I think—I think—"

Kodanth found he could no longer speak. The

orange Changeling looked down and saw the tip of the Decimaar Blade grazing his chest, its pale energies now spiraling around him.

"You think too much," said Gunmar. "So stop."

The wispy tendrils of energy crawled up Kodanth's stricken face and turned his eyes into two mirrored orbs. Gunmar removed his Decimaar Blade, and Kodanth stood still and silent before him. Skulking in the background, Dictatious wanted to whoop in joy. Instead, he forced himself to wear a more somber expression.

"Kodanth, make yourself useful for a change. March down to the pens and offer yourself to my Horde—as a meal," Gunmar suggested rather plainly.

Without protest, Kodanth turned and shambled over to the entrance of the Horde pens. The crystal spikes retracted, Kodanth descended underground, and Dictatious heard the starving Horde roar in delight.

Gunmar returned to the sand and used the Decimaar Blade to recreate the entire map as Nomura had described it to him in her whispers. Still white-hot with energy, its searing tip drew all the nine Xs that represented Skarlagk's hideouts.

"Dictatious," Gunmar said to his one remaining adviser. "I give you the honor of preparing my forces for battle."

"At once, Dark Underlord," said Dictatious with false humility. "And let me be the first to address you by your glorious new title—Gunmar the Warbringer!"

Gunmar heard the words and bared his fangs in a twisted smile.

CHAPTER 11
PLAN K

With unbridled speed, the gyre rocketed down the tunnels crisscrossing beneath the Earth. Toby, Claire, Blinky, and NotEnrique held on for dear life inside the Troll vehicle, while Draal manned the controls.

"Can you go easy on the clutch, dude?" Toby groaned, rubbing his belly.

"No," said Draal, pulling a lever and sending the gyre pinballing down another tunnel.

Toby's face turned as green as NotEnrique's before Draal slammed on the brakes, and the gyre came to an abrupt stop within an active volcano.

"Oh, boy, here come yesterday's tacos," warned Toby.

Claire shuddered as Toby leaned out of the gyre

and puked into the lava flowing beside them. A few feet ahead, the magma started to churn and swell under a slab of igneous rock, raising it upward.

"We'd better hurry or we'll miss our connecting flight," said Blinky. "So to speak."

Draal opened the gyre door and started handing heavy bundles to everyone. Claire unfolded her bundle and discovered that it was some sort of strange uniform. The suit was hewn from heavy-duty fabrics, with colorful gemstones dotting the seams. A large hollowed-out crystal sat at the top, like a helmet, with another bulky crystal attached to the back, like a scuba tank. Toby weakly wiped the side of his mouth with the back of his hand, then inspected the suit's gloves. They only had spaces for four fingers.

"I'm guessing you didn't buy these at the boutique on Delancy Street," Claire said.

"Graven Garb," said Blinky as he donned his own uniform. "AAARRRGGHH!!!'s tribe—the Krubera—designed these millennia ago to withstand the crushing pressures and absolute darkness of their deepest mines."

"Hold on a tick," NotEnrique groused. "This is

one dwarf who ain't going a-mining! Besides, I don't even see one of those Graven Garbs for me."

"Maybe the Krubera have a petites section," Toby joked while nudging NotEnrique.

"Unfortunately, RotGut only had four suits in their inventory," Blinky explained. "You'll have to share with someone."

"Not it!" said Toby, Blinky, and Draal before Claire did.

She threw her hands up in the air and said, "Fine! But that better be a fresh diaper on you!"

NotEnrique hopped into Claire's baggy suit, while the others finished dressing. The volcano rumbled, and the lava level started to rise.

"Helmets!" Draal yelled.

The group latched the hollow crystals securely to their Graven Garb and followed Draal onto the floating slab. The rock began to quake beneath their feet as the volcanic pressure built.

"Hold on to your horns," Draal said. "If you got 'em."

Without warning, the lava surged under the igneous platform, launching the team up, out of the volcano's caldera, and into a dark and weightless void.

"Um, did that volcano shoot us straight into outer space?" Toby asked.

The gemstones studding the Graven Garb suddenly glowed. The spectrum of color revealed that they had not traveled to space—but to the bottom of the ocean. From inside their watertight helmets, Toby and Claire looked down and realized that they had just erupted out of an undersea volcano.

"NotEnrique, you've got to see this!" Claire said in wonder.

But the Changeling remained clutched to her side. Claire thought she felt him shivering.

"Nope!" NotEnrique said quickly. "I'm good!"

"Welcome to the Mariana Trench!" Blinky exclaimed.

Somehow, the others could clearly hear Blinky's voice in their ears.

"Whoa!" Toby said. "These helmets have better reception than my cell phone!"

"These crystal helmets have been attuned to share the same frequency," said Blinky. "Think of them as something similar to a human child's crude communication device—the two cans connected by a string. Only without the string.

Or the cans, for that matter."

"Blinky, this is amazing," Claire said. "But why are we even here?"

"Perhaps it is time that I shared with you the *K* in my Plan K," said Blinky.

Blinky pointed above them. The group craned their heads up and stared through their crystal visors in awe. A gargantuan Deep-Sea Troll stepped over them as it walked across the ocean floor. Unlike other Trolls, its body was made of living coral, not rock, and a crust of barnacles and seaweed clung to it like a thick coat.

"Behold," announced Blinky. "The Kelpestrum!"

The Kelpestrum trod along the ocean floor, each of its footsteps kicking up huge clouds of silt.

"Oh my gosh!" Toby hyperventilated. "Oh my gosh! Oh my gosh! Oh my gosh!"

"The Kelpestrum . . . ," Draal whispered in awe. "My father used to tell me stories of him. How he's a prehistoric Deep-Sea Troll, the last of its kind. How he's related to Mountain Trolls like Gatto or Craggen and his Brothers Three. Kanjigar said the Kelpestrum doesn't care about anyone or anything. He just keeps to the seabed, always walking, always consuming everything in his path."

"Everything . . . including rare Troll artifacts," Blinky added.

Putting his four arms to use, Blinky swam toward the Kelpestrum, and the others joined him. NotEnrique still trembled inside Claire's Graven Garb, clinging tightly to her waist.

"Stop fidgeting, NotEnrique!" Claire told him. "What's the matter—scared of a little water?"

"What? Me, afraid?!" said NotEnrique.

His elfin eyes darted to the sides nervously as NotEnrique became more and more aware of the dark, deep, endless ocean around them.

"Uh, don't be silly, Nuñez!" he said, trying to sound brave. "Yer just, er, kickin' me in the gronk-nuks every time ya doggy paddle!"

"Wait, did you say *rare Troll artifacts*?" Toby asked Blinky. "You mean, there could be another Glamour Mask inside of that thing?"

"Precisely, Tobias!" said Blinky. "Legend holds that the Kelpestrum once swallowed an entire undersea Trollmarket—the factual basis for your absurd human tale of Atlantis."

"Whoa," Toby said, fogging up his visor.

"Whoa, indeed," Blinky went on. "Before they were eaten, the aquatic Troll villagers used to manufacture many powerful totems, most notably the Glamour Masks."

"So we enter the Kelpestrum, get the mask, swim back to the gyre, and return to Arcadia Oaks to convince everybody that Jim's still around, even when he isn't," said Claire, all in one breath.

"Correct," Blinky answered. "Except for the part about swimming back."

His six eyes went crossed as they watched a small crack etch along his crystal faceplate. Little drops of moisture started to bead along the fissure and dribble into his helmet.

"It appears these Graven Garb might not handle the oceans as well as they handle the mines!" Blinky worried. "Perhaps RotGut sold us defective models."

"Or cheap knockoffs!" said NotEnrique's voice from somewhere around Claire's midsection.

"In either case, I fear they won't last much longer at these depths!" Blinky added as everyone's suits started to take on water.

CHAPTER 12
THE CRYSTAL SPIRE

Hours later, Skarlagk's hollowness still hung over Jim like an extra suit of cold and heavy armor. He had left Skarlagk and her generals to plan their attack on Gunmar's Crucible Pit, and he had explored more of the fortress. Ascending to the highest spire, Jim found a small room containing what appeared to be a crystal collection. Numerous gems lined the tower's shelves, with chalk markings written around them.

"Looks like Skarlagk's been digging for Triumbric Stones of her own," Jim said.

Scanning the shelves, Jim's eyes landed on a hunk of emerald-like crystal. It shone with the same eerie green glow that permeated everything else in the Darklands. The glow called to the Trollhunter, bringing him closer.

Finding some beat-up gem-cutting tools nearby, he took the emerald from the shelf and set it carefully on a worktable. Following the methods that Vendel had taught him only weeks ago, Jim used the tools to carve the green stone. He concentrated, chiseling along the ridges, cleaving off the dull parts, and losing himself in the task. When he was done, Jim held up a brilliant emerald shard in the palm of his hand.

"I wonder if . . . ," Jim began, looking down at the space where his Amulet used to be.

As if in response, a compartment in the empty circle opened to accept the gem, just as the Amulet had done with the Triumbric Stones. Jim inserted the shard and watched the engravings on his Eclipse Armor suddenly shift to neon green. The effect only lasted for a second before the red returned. Yet Jim still felt somehow . . . *different* with this new stone loaded into his armor. Before he could even guess as to why, a flaming foot kicked open the metal door behind him.

"HANDS!" shouted Rob as he barged into the tower, ready to throw flames. "Show me your hands, creep, unless you want me to drop you like the rest of Doctor Despot's goons!"

Jim instinctively raised his hands like he'd been caught doing something illegal, then remembered who he was dealing with.

"Rob, for the last time, there is no Doctor Despot, and you are not Gun Robot!" Jim griped.

"Your answer scans as true on Gun Robot's lie detector," said Rob in his robot voice.

The Heetling then did a somersault and sprang back up by the spire's open window, as if searching for intruders. He looked down at the Nyarlagroth queen carrying them—and the rest of Skarlagk's mobile base—over a dune of gray gravel.

"What happened to you back at the labyrinth?" Jim asked.

"Well, after we got separated, I went back through the maze, trying to retrace your steps," Rob explained. "But I must've taken a left when I should've gone right. Anyway, long story short, I found the shish-kebabed Nyarlagroth, followed the Gumm-Gumm footsteps leading away from it, and tracked the slime trails left behind by their rides. Ta-da!"

Rob then leaned closer to Jim and whispered, "By the way, I'd watch out with Skarlagk. She's got more loose screws that Gun Robot after his cage match with—"

"Yeah, yeah, I get the picture," Jim said, waving away Rob. "Although my first clue was probably the way she carries her father's severed head in her purse."

"I see you've found my Crystal Spire," came a female Gumm-Gumm voice from behind them.

Jim froze in place, while a wide grin danced across Rob's flaming face.

"Jim, you know that part in *Gun Robot 3*?" Rob asked. "When Gun Robot's partner bad-mouths their lieutenant—only to turn around and find out that the lieutenant's been right behind him the whole time, listening to everything he said? *This* is just like that!"

Jim winced in embarrassment. Sure enough, Skarlagk loomed humorlessly behind him.

"I, uh . . . I'm sorry, Skarlagk," Jim said with a dry cough.

"Worse has been said about me, I assure you," Skarlagk replied before tossing what looked like a leather pouch into Jim's hands. "Drink."

Jim felt liquid swirling around inside of it, like a

canteen, and looked up at Skarlagk with gratitude in his eyes.

"Is this water?" Jim asked.

"More or less," Skarlagk answered.

That was good enough for Jim. He removed the cap at the end and drank deeply. It tasted slightly salty and sour, but at least it was wet. With each chug, Jim's throat soothed and his headache faded. He drained the pouch of its contents, his long thirst now quenched.

"Thank you," Jim said as he tried to return the canteen to Skarlagk.

"That bladder is yours to keep," said Skarlagk.

"I'm sorry, did you say *bladder*?!" Jim asked, now holding the pouch at arm's length from his disgusted face. "You cleaned this thing out before giving it to me . . . right?"

"More or less," Skarlagk answered again. "But we have more pressing matters ahead of us. Even now, the Nyarlagroth queen moves my compound ever closer to Gunmar's. Soon, you and I shall unite behind the power of your Eclipse Armor and eradicate the Skullcrusher from this and every other world."

"And just before you finish him off, I'll deliver an awesome closing line," added Rob. "Like 'Pop goes the Gunmar!' Or 'You've just been Trollhunted!'"

Skarlagk and Jim just stared at Rob before resuming their conversation. Not that Rob seemed to mind. He turned back into a fireball and began bouncing around the tower.

"Okay, Skarlagk," Jim resumed. "I swear. And once Gunmar's out of the way, we will locate the Changeling nursery and free Enrique."

Skarlagk regarded Jim as if he was crazy and asked, "Why would we ever do that?"

"To, um, save all the babies that are trapped in there?" said Jim not quite understanding the question.

"Ah, you misunderstand, Trollhunter," Skarlagk answered. "You cannot free anyone from the Changeling nursery, for it—and everything inside it—will be burned to the ground."

"WHAT?!" Jim roared, the engraved lines in his Eclipse Armor also flaring in outrage. "I can't believe what I'm hearing! You actually expect me to . . . to . . ."

The Trollhunter took a deep breath, centering

himself. Even his armor seemed to cool as he calmed down and tried speaking again.

"Skarlagk," Jim resumed. "I think it's you who misunderstood me. I could never, ever agree to hurting anything as innocent as a child. There has to be another way."

"There is no other way," Skarlagk said without hesitation. "I will not rest until every last trace of Gunmar—including the Changeling nursery—has been obliterated from existence."

"Then you'll have to do it over my dead body," Jim vowed as the Sword of Eclipse manifested in his hand.

He twirled the blade once to loosen his wrist, readying to battle, if need be. Skarlagk calmly removed two spears from her quiver and said, "I am prepared to make that sacrifice—and many more—in pursuit of my revenge."

She sharpened her spearheads against each other, grinding out sparks with each scrape. The embers caught Rob's attention as he ping-ponged across the tower. He finally came to a stop in his humanoid form between Jim and Skarlagk.

"Whoa, you can cut the tension in here with a

bone saw, amiright?" Rob joked. "But seriously, folks, this's just like the time Gun Robot and Sally-Go-Back fought in—"

"Not. Now," Jim warned, far from laughing.

"Know that you will not have died in vain, Trollhunter," Skarlagk said. "For once I rip the Sword of Eclipse from your lifeless hand, I will use it to finish Gunmar in the way that you clearly could not."

Jim tightened his fingers around his sword. Skarlagk did the same with her spears. With their brief pact dissolved, the Trollhunter and Gumm-Gumm charged at each other. But before their weapons could clash, a thunderous explosion rocked the entire fortress.

"Fire in the hole!" yelled Rob as the shockwave sent him and Jim to the quaking floor.

Another blast hit the spire, punching a large smoking hole through the wall. Skarlagk rushed over to it and gaped outside. The spears slipped out of her hands and dropped onto the cinders at her feet.

"Not yet," were the only words Skarlagk could muster.

Jim ran over to the smoldering crater and looked out. The color drained from his face.

"Oh no," said Jim.

Peering through the hole, down the tower, and across the Darklands' unforgiving terrain, Jim saw an immense Gumm-Gumm army overtake Skarlagk's fortress. Thousands of soldiers swarmed the recoiling Nyarlagroth queen and began climbing the walls built on her back with axes and grappling hooks. At the same time, Gumm-Gumm archers shot flaming arrows, while the biggest catapults Jim had ever seen launched blazing green boulders.

"It's Gunmar," Skarlagk finally admitted. "He's ambushed us."

Moving with impressive speed for a Troll of her size, Skarlagk grabbed Rob by his sizzling neck and clamped down. If his flames hurt her calloused hands, Skarlagk didn't show it.

"You!" she hissed. "You told them where to find us! That's what you were up to before your convenient arrival just now!"

"You—GAK!—got it all wrong!" said Rob as he gasped for air. "Gun Robot ain't—URK!—no punk informer!"

Jim vanished his Sword of Eclipse and tried to get between Skarlagk and Rob, whose fire was dimming without oxygen.

"Skarlagk, stop!" Jim shouted. "This won't solve anything! The only way we'll have even a *chance* of surviving this is if we stick togeth—"

He never got to finish the thought. Another molten boulder smashed through the wall, sending the Trollhunter plummeting out of the spire and to his doom.

CHAPTER 13
SUNK

"Okay, let's keep calm," said Claire as water continued to pour into her Graven Garb. "Just focus on getting inside the Kelpestrum. Once we've got the mask, I can teleport us back to the gyre with my Shadow Staff."

"And there's our way in!" Draal yelled as his visor started to buckle too.

He pointed his metal arm at a set of giant gills on the Kelpestrum's neck. The slits were each at least ten feet tall, and they fluttered open and closed as the Deep-Sea Troll breathed in and out. Following Draal's lead, the group swam closer to the Kelpestrum's gills.

"Um, are we sure this's gonna work?" questioned Toby.

Before anyone could answer, the gills reopened, and a powerful current sucked them all inside the Kelpestrum.

Everything went dark and topsy-turvy as they passed through the Troll's respiratory system. To Toby, it felt like he was going down the world's most dangerous water-flume ride, but with all the lights turned off. Then, a tremendous flood of seawater deposited Draal, Blinky, Toby, NotEnrique, and Claire's bodies in a heap within the Kelpestrum.

"Ugh," groaned NotEnrique as he shimmied up to share Claire's visor. "Now I know what toilet paper feels like after it's been flushed!"

"Please, no more—URP!—potty talk." Toby belched as he held his queasy stomach. "I'm still not over that taco incident in the gyre. Super—URP!—*no bueno!*"

The teammates helped one another up—it was a bit of a struggle with their bulky Graven Garb—and got their bearings. The gems on their suits lit up in the darkness, illuminating the air-filled cavern. Blinky held his four hands against the damp algae-covered walls and felt them rise and fall in a steady rhythm.

"We appear to be in his gullet," Blinky marveled. "Now it's just a matter of searching the entire Kelpestrum from stem to stern—over and over again, if need be—until we find that scarcest of Troll relics: the extraordinarily unique Glamour Ma—"

"Hey, are those some over here?" Toby asked, pointing down at, like, ten Glamour Masks floating in the water around his feet.

"Oh. Well, that was remarkably easy," Blinky said.

"Way to go, Tobes!" Claire cheered as she scooped up all the masks before Toby could. "But you'd better let *me* hold them. No offense."

"None taken!" said Toby, receiving four pats on the back from Blinky, plus two stronger ones from Draal. "Just between us fleshbags, I was feelin' pretty guilty about dropping that last Glamour Mask! I thought I'd really let Jim down and doomed . . . us . . . all. . . ."

Claire, NotEnrique, Blinky, and Draal all squinted at Toby as his voice trailed off and his eyes grew wide. They turned around and immediately saw why he was having trouble forming new words. Dozens and dozens of Volcanic Trolls crept out from the Kelpestrum's innards, their weapons all trained on the trespassers.

"Volcanic Trolls!" Toby finally said. "I thought these guys only hung around Gatto!"

"I'm afraid they infest all giant Trolls, like mindless parasites," Blinky explained.

Claire handed the masks to Blinky, pulled out her Shadow Staff, and extended it. The handle darkened as she prepared to teleport everyone out of the Kelpestrum.

"Get ready to shadow-jump, gang!" Claire said.

But before she could open a black hole, a Volcanic Troll reached out and snatched the staff from her hands.

"Hey!" Claire and NotEnrique yelled at the same time. "Give that back!"

They went after her Shadow Staff, but several more Volcanic Trolls spilled into the Kelpestrum's gullet, blocking them. Blinky and Draal stood protectively in front of Claire and NotEnrique, while Toby unstrapped his Warhammer from his Graven Garb.

"I already failed my best friend once today," Toby said, his eyes set in determination. "We're getting out of here with these Glamour Masks, even if I have to fight every single, last one of you Volcanic Trolls."

As the mute Volcanic Trolls closed in, Draal cracked his knuckles and grinned. He took another step forward ahead of Blinky and said, "Now *that* sounds like my kind of escape plan!"

CHAPTER 14
THE HORDE UNLEASHED

Across the Dunes of Desolation, Gunmar watched his legions of Gumm-Gumms descend upon Skarlagk's nomadic castle. Even from this distance, he could hear his line of catapults smashing the fortress walls.

"The siege goes as planned, Dark Underlord," Dictatious reported as he clambered up to the top of the same dune where Gunmar stood. "Soon, Skarlagk's rebellion will be extinguished, and your rule of the Darklands shall be absolute."

"That's not enough," Gunmar said. "I want that traitorous grunt to suffer, just as her father suffered. Release . . . my Horde."

"By your command, Warbringer," said Dictatious before he cupped his four hands over his mouth and blew a piercing whistle that carried over the dunes.

At the frontlines of battle, the Gumm-Gumms heard Dictatious's signal and wheeled forward several oversized cages made from those same orange crystal spikes. The spikes retracted and the Gumm-Gumms stood clear as Gunmar's Horde burst out of their confines. Hundreds of Helheetis, Stalklings, and Antramonstrum galloped, flew, and spread across the battlefield toward the rebel fortress.

"Sire, it's . . . breathtaking!" exclaimed Dictatious from their dune. "After centuries of planning—of smuggling young Helheetis, Stalklings, and Antramonstrum from the surface through the Fetches—your Horde runs wild!"

"And they say nothing grows in the Darklands," Gunmar mused as the rebel alarms rang.

The airborne Stalklings were the first to strike Skarlagk's stronghold. With earsplitting screams, the Vulture Trolls dive-bombed the rebel base, nearly knocking down the tallest tower—and Jim along with it.

The Trollhunter hung on to the side of the spire from a pair of brand-new whips. Crackling with neon green energy, they first appeared in Jim's flailing hands as he fell toward certain death. The whips had surged out of the Eclipse Armor, courtesy of the emerald gem in his chest plate. Reacting on pure survival instinct, Jim swung the whips blindly, managing to wrap them around the flagpole atop the tower. He dangled there, breathless, but alive.

"Seriously?!" Jim shouted as another Vulture Troll buzzed him. "Stalklings? How could this day get any worse?"

Looking down, Jim saw scores of Gumm-Gumms grappling up the tower toward him.

"Boy, I really fell into that one, didn't I?" Jim asked rhetorically.

Left with nowhere to go, the Trollhunter saw another incoming airstrike. Jim loosened one of the whips from the flagpole and lashed it toward the swooping Vulture Troll. The fluorescent whip cracked through the air and fastened around the Stalkling's beak. Releasing the second whip from the flagpole, Jim held on to the first for dear life. The Vulture Troll pulled him off the tower and away from the Gumm-Gumms who had nearly snagged him.

As the Stalkling spiraled out of control, Jim started to feel airsick. Ignoring his nausea, he arced the second whip forward and wrapped it, too, around the creature's beak. Jim pulled himself onto its back and started to tug left and right on his whips, piloting the Stalkling as he had seen Skarlagk pilot her Nyarlagroth.

"Oh, Tobes, if you could see me now!" Jim exclaimed, finally feeling in control again.

But Jim's smile faded just as quickly as it had appeared. Once again, he forced himself not to think of his best friend or any of the others he'd left behind.

No time for stuff like that, Jim thought as he looked at the chaos below him. *This is war.*

Pulling down on his whips, Jim drove the Stalkling lower. They skimmed across the top of the battlefield, with Jim staying low on the Vulture Troll's back to avoid detection. Using the whips as reins, Jim guided the Stalkling over Gumm-Gumms' armored heads, under swinging catapult arms, and between barrages of blazing arrows. Now yanking up on the whips, Jim arced the Stalkling over Skarlagk's besieged fortress.

"Thanks for the joyride," Jim shouted. "But here's where I get off."

The Trollhunter slid his whips off the Stalkling's beak and jumped clear of its back. The Vulture Troll watched Jim land safely on one of the obsidian ramparts—right before it flew smack into the rebel flag flapping on the tower. The flag ripped from the pole and enveloped the Stalkling. Unable to see, it crashed into one of the catapults which, in turn, knocked into another catapult.

From the fortress's roof, Jim watched more catapults tip over and into one another, like a row of dominoes. The Gumm-Gumms manning them fled in terror as the catapults' flaming boulders set fire to the overturned war machines.

"Um, that works," Jim said of the chain reaction he had accidentally started.

Looking into the fortress's inner ward, Jim spotted Skarlagk. She fought off a bunch of Gunmar's soldiers with one hand while keeping Rob in a chokehold with the other. His flames flickered as he started to pass out.

"I can't believe I'm about to do this," Jim moaned to himself.

He wrapped one of his whips around a nearby parapet, then used it like a rope to rappel down the fortress wall. Reaching the ward, Jim unfastened his whip, only to be nearly devoured by a lunging Helheeti.

The large fire-cat dug its blazing claws into the turf and spun around for another attack. One of Skarlagk's rebels foolishly tried to stab the Helheeti with his long ax, but only succeeded in splitting it into two separate beasts.

"No!" cried Jim. "The only way to defeat a Helheeti is to put out its flames!"

But his warning came too late, as the pair of Helheetis pounced on the Gumm-Gumm. Jim turned away from the grisly scene and surveyed the area. He spotted a bunch of those stone bowls the rebels used to boil Nyarlagroth eggs—right under a sturdy trough filled with water.

The Helheetis licked their burning chops as they pawed closer to Jim. He wanted to lead them closer to the trough, but how? Jim looked down and remembered the whips in his hands.

"I really hope this works," Jim said as more explosions and shouts sounded behind him.

He flicked his whip at one of the Helheetis, and the neon line cinched around the fire-cat as if it were solid.

"Now that's crispy!" Jim shouted before whipping the second Helheeti.

The flaming felines struggled to break free of their new leashes, but Jim didn't let go. Pulling as hard as he could, the Trollhunter dragged the fire-cats over to the trough and kicked it over. The water splashed over the Helheetis and converted them to steam.

"No!" Rob wheezed under Skarlagk's choke-hold. "That Helheeti was my momma!"

Jim rolled his eyes and broke into a sprint toward Skarlagk. Several more of her armed rebels tried to stop Jim. He just whipped them away, never breaking his stride.

Skarlagk single-handedly flattened another phalanx of Gunmar's soldiers before she heard a loud *CRACK* in the air. Skarlagk turned and saw the Trollhunter behind her, readying his emerald whips for another swing.

"That first one was a warning, Skarlagk," Jim said. "Believe me, I don't like Rob either. But if you don't let go of him now, my next whip won't miss."

Skarlagk released Rob, who collapsed to the ground, unconscious. She and Jim then began circling each other, weapons at the ready. Their bodies reflected on a massive chunk of obsidian beside them, which had fallen from the shattered rampart above them.

"We don't have to do this," Jim pleaded. "We can still team up and stop Gunmar without hurting any innocents."

"There are no innocents in the Darklands," Skarlagk said before she thrust her spears.

Jim dodged, spun around, and swiped with his whips. They noosed around Skarlagk, pinning her arms to her sides. She strained to reach her quiver of spears. But the whips sizzled with a fluorescent charge of electricity, stunning Skarlagk.

"Please," Jim said. "I don't want to fight you."

Jim let his whips go slack, and Skarlagk shrugged them off. She fixed an angry glare at the Trollhunter.

"I know you hate Gunmar," said Jim. "I hate him too. But if you destroy the nursery, how does that make you any better than him?"

Skarlagk's eyes softened as Jim's words hit her. She looked at the war around them. Her rebels clashed against Gumm-Gumm soldiers. Nets fired from the parapets and downed more Stalklings. Helheetis multiplied into greater and greater numbers and burned everything they touched. Skarlagk had spent most of her life preparing for this confrontation, yet she felt no satisfaction.

"Where does it stop?" Jim asked. "With your own destruction? Because Gunmar definitely had a hand in making you the Troll you are today, whether you admit it or not."

"I . . . I don't . . . ," Skarlagk began to say, before the weakened wall behind her detonated. Fire and debris rained down on the ward, and the impact knocked over Skarlagk, sending her spears flying out of their quiver. The entire fortress ground to a shuddering halt as the Nyarlagroth queen stopped moving altogether.

Jim and Skarlagk coughed, until they saw something else start to move in the smoke. Two Antramonstrum probed into the breech like a pair of living clouds. They passed over fallen rebels and Gumm-Gumms alike, reducing the bodies to skeletons under their acidic touch.

Skarlagk's eyes widened as she saw the Antramonstrum drift in her direction. She crawled under a pile of Gumm-Gumms she had beaten, but Jim had nowhere to run. He backed into the chunk of obsidian behind him and tried to climb it, but his hands found nothing to grasp on the smooth black surface. Jim was cornered.

And the Antramonstrum surged closer, dissolving everything in their paths.

CHAPTER 15
A HOLE MESS OF TROUBLE

If Toby and Claire had ever questioned why Draal was called "the Deadly," he answered that in less than thirty seconds. That's how long it took him to take out every single Volcanic Troll surrounding them.

First, Draal tucked his body into a ball and rolled smack into the front line of Volcanic Trolls, toppling them like tenpins. In one swift motion, the son of Kanjigar then flipped into the air and caught two of the many weapons those Volcanic Trolls had just lost. When he landed, Draal held a double ax in his mechanical hand and a short sword in his other.

"These'll do," Draal smirked before launching back into the fray.

Swinging his blades with the skill that comes

from a lifetime of training in the Hero's Forge, Draal shred his way through the Volcanic Trolls. He struck blow after blow against them, denting their metal helmets, snapping their weapons in two, and slamming their bodies to the ground. And Draal did all this with a smile, laughing maniacally the whole time.

"Ha-HA!" Draal boomed as he punched out the last Volcanic Troll. "How'd I do?"

"Great Gronka Morka," said Blinky, Toby, Claire, and NotEnrique in unison.

They all stared at Draal—sorta impressed and sorta freaked out—before gazing down at the beaten Volcanic Trolls littering the gullet in his wake. Blinky then shook the stunned look from his face and answered, "Twenty-eight-point-five seconds, Draal. A new personal best!"

But a subtle movement in the periphery caught Claire's attention. The groggy Volcanic Troll with her stolen Shadow Staff got up and stumbled down a passageway.

"Hey!" Claire called out to her teammates, getting their attention. "There goes our only way outta here!"

To make matters worse, a second wave of

Volcanic Trolls started filing into the chamber.

"Draal cleared us a path," Toby said as he hefted his Warhammer. "Now let's use it!"

Toby swung his enchanted mallet into the onslaught of Volcanic Trolls, sending them flying in all directions. With his arms full of Glamour Masks, Blinky kicked at a few more of their enemy. And Claire bolted in the direction of the one holding her Shadow Staff.

But a large brute of a Volcanic Troll intercepted her midway, grabbing Claire by the wrists and lifting her off the ground.

"Well," Claire said. "This's the last mistake you'll ever make."

The brute looked down as Claire's Graven Garb unzipped down the middle, and NotEnrique's yellow eyes peeked out at him.

"Surprise!" yelled NotEnrique before he jumped out of Claire's suit and onto the Volcanic Troll's face. The brute immediately released Claire and tried to pull NotEnrique away.

"Go, Nuñez!" the little Changeling shouted at Claire while clawing at the Volcanic Troll.

"*Gracias*, NotEnrique!" Claire called over her

shoulder as she took off again.

Claire dove past Draal as he took on another squad of Volcanic Trolls, then clambered into the Kelpestrum's next chamber. To cover Claire's escape, Toby stood in front of the passage and twirled the Warhammer in front of him like a propeller.

"Back off, you lame-o lava losers!" Toby said heroically to the Volcanic Trolls. "Unless you want to taste the sweet smack of justice from my Warham—"

Toby's spinning Warhammer got wedged between the passageway's two rocky walls. He pulled on it with all his might, but the weapon remained stuck in place. The Volcanic Trolls cocked their heads in confusion.

"Um, hold on a sec," Toby grunted as he yanked on the Warhammer. "You know what would be cool? If this thing would shrink down like Claire's Shadow Staff!"

"I'll get right on that!" Blinky yelled as he kicked away more Volcanic Trolls. "Provided we survive this experience!"

Inside the passage, the narrow walls throbbed

with the Kelpestrum's heartbeat as Claire slid between them. Spotting the Volcanic Troll with her Shadow Staff dead ahead, she poured on the speed. Claire pushed her legs as fast as they could go, jumped, and tackled the Volcanic Troll. They both tumbled into a new section of the Kelpestrum, where slimy mucus dripped from the stalactites above them. As Claire got to her feet, NotEnrique, Blinky, Toby, and Draal rushed up behind her.

"Uh, more enemy reinforcements right behind us!" Toby said in a panic. "It's like the Kelpestrum filled up at an all-you-can-eat Volcanic-Troll buffet!"

Claire held out an open hand toward the Volcanic Troll who was holding her staff. There was no other way out of this segment of the Kelpestrum other than the passageway behind her and her friends. The sounds of the third, fourth, and possibly fifth waves of Volcanic Trolls grew closer.

"Hand it over," Claire demanded. "Now."

Trapped, the Volcanic Troll started to return the Shadow Staff, when the soft, marshy floor below all of them suddenly trembled. A loud gurgling noise soon followed, reverberating off the snot-plastered walls. Warm water sloshed around their ankles.

"Uhhh." Toby grimaced. "That sounds a lot like the sounds we heard inside Gatto. Before we, uh, *evacuated* his Keep, if you catch my drift."

"I'm afraid you're only half right, Tobias," Blinky said over another gurgle. "In our foot chase through the Kelpestrum, we've inadvertently arrived next to a far different part of its anatomy!"

As three of his arms clutched tightly to the Glamour Masks, a fourth pointed straight up at the high ceiling. Between the dripping stalactites, a ring of muscle relaxed and opened.

"A blowhole!" Blinky shouted before the loudest gurgle yet drowned out his voice.

NotEnrique had just enough time to leap back into Claire's Graven Garb and zip it shut. With a sudden jolt, the chamber around them contracted, and a forceful rush of air jettisoned them, Blinky, Toby, Draal, and the Volcanic Troll out of the Kelpestrum's blowhole.

Their bodies plunged into the ocean's cold, murky depths. The tide yanked the Glamour Masks from Blinky's arms, while water started pouring into everyone's suits once again.

"We don't have much time!" said Blinky as he

fumbled for the sinking masks. "In a few seconds, we won't be any better off than that Volcanic Troll!"

Without a Graven Garb of his own, the Volcanic Troll immediately went limp outside of the relative safety of the Kelpestrum. His body sank away from the others—just as the Shadow Staff fell out of his fingers.

"No!" Claire shouted before diving after her staff.

Blinky, Draal, and Toby tried to swim after her, but their crystal helmets started to splinter under the pressure.

"Perhaps I shall join you soon enough, Father," Draal said as another long fracture formed across his helmet's visor. "I only wish we had not failed our current Trollhunter."

"We haven't yet!" Claire responded as she kicked after her Shadow Staff. Ignoring the cobweb of cracks spreading across her own helmet, she reached for the staff, but it was just out of her grasp.

"Can't reach!" she strained. "The water in the suit—it's slowing me down!"

"No kiddin'!" NotEnrique said, trying to keep his head above the water pooling into her boot.

"C'mon, Nuñez! Think of something! We can't go out like this! *I* can't go out like this!"

"I don't know what to do!" Claire yelled, thinking of Jim locking her out of the vault, wondering if that would truly be the last time she saw him. "My arm's just not long enough!"

NotEnrique spit out saltwater and said, "On it!"

The soaked Changeling squirmed up Claire's leg, past her ribs, and along her outstretched arm. Standing on her palm, NotEnrique extended his body, and the baggy Graven Garb sleeve elongated. His little green hands filled two of the four finger slots of Claire's glove—and snagged the Shadow Staff.

"Yes!" Claire cheered. "You did it, NotEnrique! And here I thought you were afraid of the water."

"What?! Don't be ridiculous, I ain't afraid of no water," NotEnrique groused before he lowered his voice so Claire couldn't hear. "Just of swimmin' in it. . . ."

Now in command of her Shadow Staff once again, Claire opened a black hole in the middle of the ocean and swam through it. A new portal opened up under Blinky, Draal, and Toby, whose suits were collapsing around them.

Back inside the undersea volcano, a third, much larger shadow portal opened, dumping Claire, NotEnrique, Toby, Blinky, and Draal next to the gyre—along with hundreds of gallons of seawater. The deluge hit the magma, creating tremendous billows of steam.

Everyone removed their stressed helmets and watched them shatter in their hands.

"I believe the appropriate human expression for a moment such as this would be: 'Does anyone have a change of pants?'" said Blinky, still visibly shaken from the ordeal.

"Good thing I came prepared," NotEnrique said as he wiggled out of Claire's Graven Garb and pointed at his diaper.

"Nice save!" said Toby as he helped Claire into the gyre, her body too exhausted to move on its own. "You okay?"

"No," Claire admitted, her voice weak. "But if this helps Jim, it was worth it."

"Alas, all the Glamour Masks slipped from my hands as we passed through the Kelpestrum's blowhole," Blinky said, his head turned down in dismay.

Everyone stared at him in shock, until he looked up with a smile. Blinky held up his four hands, which clutched a single Glamour Mask.

"Except for this one," Blinky added with a wink.

"Awesomesauce!" said Toby. "Can I hold it?"

"NO!" everyone else shouted at once.

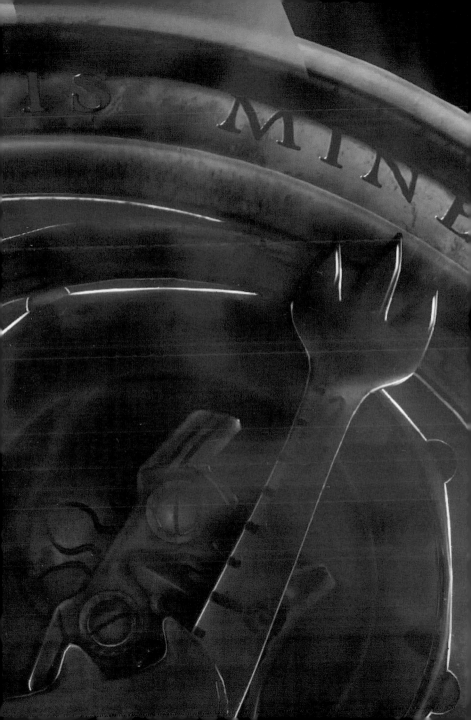

CHAPTER 16
CONSUMED BY REVENGE

Jim snapped his whips at the Antramonstrum. But the sparking green lines just passed ineffectively through the two clouds as they converged toward him. Now officially out of options, Jim raised his arms protectively. The shield automatically fanned out of his gauntlet, covering his face, and the flaring red lines that shot through his armor went completely dark.

The Antramonstrum stopped mere inches in front of Jim. With his Eclipse Armor now all-black, Jim's camouflaged body blended seamlessly into the obsidian behind him. To the mindless Antramonstrum, it was as if the Trollhunter had simply disappeared into thin air. The confused death clouds backed away from the sheer volcanic glass, passing over the pile of Gumm-Gumms. Jim lowered his shield and opened one eye. The Antramonstrum were gone.

"This thing's full of surprises today!" Jim marveled at his Eclipse Armor as the red lines piped through it once again.

Jim was startled when Skarlagk, also unharmed, emerged from under what was now a pile of skeletons. The two survivors shared a silent nod before they heard a roar of voices build outside of the fortress. Just beyond the walls, Gumm-Gumms banged their war drums and repeated the same battle cry over and over again.

"GUNMAR! GUNMAR! GUNMAR!"

"He's coming!" said Skarlagk while reaching for her spears.

But her quiver was still empty, its spears lost within the rubble littering her ward. Skarlagk and Jim looked at each other as the Gumm-Gumm's chant grew louder and closer.

"The armory," Skarlagk said to Jim. "Follow me!"

She ran full-bore into her ruined fortress's keep, and Jim trailed after her. Along the way, he passed Rob, who the Antramonstrum had ignored. Jim flicked his whip, snared Rob's ankle, and dragged him into the fortress too.

No sooner had they left the ward than the Gumm-Gumm army stormed into it. The vanguard of soldiers parted, allowing Gunmar the Warbringer into the castle he just conquered. Dictatious kept close behind his Dark Underlord, rubbing his four hands together in malice.

"Search the premises!" Gunmar barked at his forces. "Look under every broken shield, if you must, but do not stop until you bring me Skarlagk's head!"

Rob stirred and found Jim propping up his body with his armored shoulder as they hurried down a spiral staircase. The Trollhunter winced at the renewed heat coming off Rob, but still refused to leave him behind.

"My hero," Rob said dreamily to Jim. "If it's all right with you, I'd like to now sing the ballad from our hit soundtrack—'This Robot's Heart (Is Programmed for Love).'"

Jim threw Rob off his body and caught up with Skarlagk at the base of the steps. He tried to keep a mental map of their surroundings as they went and guessed that they were at the very bottom of the fortress.

"In here," Skarlagk beckoned as she flung open a reinforced door with a resounding clang. Jim and Rob followed Skarlagk inside, their eyes bugging at the racks upon racks of barbaric rebel weapons around them. Skarlagk slid a heavy bolt across the door, locking it.

"Grab any weapon you like," she said while picking up a mace and a saw-toothed sword.

"Uh, I think I'm good," Jim replied, looking down at the fluorescent whips looped in his hands. "But does it really matter? Those Gumm-Gumms out there must outnumber us a thousand to one! How are we supposed to fight all of them and take on Gunmar?"

"And this time, *it's personal*," Rob added randomly.

"Once again, you misunderstand me, Trollhunter," said Skarlagk. "*We* aren't going to fight Gunmar."

She stomped her booted foot onto the stone floor—three stomps, this time—and the weapons began rattling in their racks. Without warning, a Nyarlagroth burst through the armory walls, heeding Skarlagk's call. Numerous Gumm-Gumm spears and arrows jutted from its sides like needles in a pincushion.

"I don't get it," Rob said while jerking a thumb at the Nyarlagroth. "Is this thing supposed to fight Gunmar? Because that's just ridiculous."

Skarlagk signaled the Nyarlagroth, and it obediently opened its jaws. Hauling back her leg, Skarlagk then punted Rob inside the eel's maw with a swift kick to Rob's rear.

"Catch you in the sequel!" Rob said before being swallowed in one giant gulp.

Jim looked from the slithering behemoth to Skarlagk in utter disbelief.

"What're you doing?!" Jim demanded, his whips now crackling with neon fury.

Skarlagk signaled the eel again and answered, "Saying farewell, Jim Lake Junior."

This Nyarlagroth's glowing tongue shot past its rows of teeth and slipknotted around Jim. His whips fizzled as he railed in futility against the glowing appendage. Jim could hear Gunmar's advance soldiers marching down the spiral staircase toward the armory.

"Skarlagk," Jim gasped. "You don't have to do this alone!"

"Find the nursery, Trollhunter," Skarlagk said.

As the tongue reeled Jim toward the Nyarlagroth, he watched Skarlagk. She removed her father's skull and fit it on top of her own head like a helmet of bone. Now done with the satchel, Skarlagk tossed it past Jim, and into the eel's waiting mouth.

"Rescue this 'Enrique' and the other babes within it," said Skarlagk. "Give them the childhood that Gunmar stole from me."

"Wait!" Jim shouted. "WAIT!"

The last thing he saw before the Nyarlagroth's drooling jaws shut around him was the Warrior Queen taking up her mace and sword once again. Now lodged in the cramped recesses of the throat, Jim couldn't see anything. But he could still hear just fine, even as the Nyarlagroth started to slither out of the fortress. Pressing his ear to the slippery membranes lining its insides, Jim listened to the Gumm-Gumms batter down the armory door.

"Skarlagk the Scorned," said a cruel voice.

Jim recognized it immediately. Even though it was muffled by the Nyarlagroth's body, the sound of Gunmar speaking sent chills down Jim's spine—just as it had done when he first heard it months ago.

"Hiding in a corner, just as she did when I beheaded her father," Gunmar continued. "Perhaps I shall do the same now and make a matching set of their skulls."

Jim heard another distant voice laugh and compliment his Dark Underlord's wit. The Trollhunter writhed and kicked against the tongue, but it only tightened. Even in the dark, Jim felt his vision fade as he started to black out again.

"Or perhaps I shall use my Decimaar Blade to make her finally obey my every order," said Gunmar, his voice even farther away as the Nyarlagroth burrowed out of the armory.

"I would sooner die than serve you again," came Skarlagk's faint, but ever defiant, voice.

Jim barely heard Skarlagk grunt, then drop her mace and sword, before he succumbed to the darkness.

CHAPTER 17
BURNED

When Jim woke up, it was to the thick smell of smoke and the sting of stomach acid on his armor. He scrambled to an upright position—at least as upright as the low ceiling of the Nyarlagroth's stomach allowed Jim to stand. In that moment, the Trollhunter realized two things. One, that the great eel was busy digesting Jim while he was (thankfully) unconscious. And two, that Jim could actually see in the stomach.

He looked over his shoulder and found Rob sitting dejectedly on top of a catapult boulder in the middle of a pool of churning yellow acid. He almost looked like a little kid in a time-out as he flicked tiny fireballs against the stomach walls, to no effect.

"Hey," said an unusually sullen Rob. "Glad to see

you're up. I was just about to give ya CPR. As a duly deputized robo-officer of the Future Police, I'm fully programmed in mouth-to-mouth resuscitation."

"Gee, thanks, 'Gun Robot,'" Jim said. "Or you could just burn your way out of this Nyarlagroth's gut and take me with you? Like how I saved you back at Skarlagk's fortress?"

Saying her name instantly reminded Jim of Skarlagk . . . and of her ultimate fate at Gunmar's hands. He still hadn't seen Gunmar, and yet the Trollhunter now hated the Gumm-Gumm warlord more than ever.

"I tried," Rob murmured. "But wouldn't ya know it? Turns out Nyarlagroths are fireproof on the outside *and* the inside."

Jim looked down at his legs. The Eclipse Armor protected them from the stomach's corrosive juices, yet he didn't know how long that would last—or how much breathable oxygen was left in there. With a thought, Jim vanished the whips that had become tangled about his body, while conjuring the Sword of Eclipse in his right hand.

"Okay," Jim said to Rob as he pointed the blade at the intestinal wall. "This is gonna get messy."

The Nyarlagroth lumbered past Madness Canyon, until its tubular body spasmed and bellowed out an anguished screech. The Sword of Eclipse poked through the eel from the inside and sliced a slit across its flesh. Jim and Rob then wriggled out of the incision, along with several other partially digested contents from the Nyarlagroth's belly.

"The! Dark! Lands! Suck!" muttered Jim as he wiped eel ooze from his armor.

The Nyarlagroth continued past the canyon. Jim watched with surprise as its side stitched itself back together, fully healed within seconds.

"Those things are as tough as they are ugly," said Rob.

Rob held out his hand for a high-five, but Jim pretended he didn't see it.

"Look, Rob, back there with the Helheetis I stopped," Jim began, searching for the right words. "I, um . . . well, I'm sorry about your mom."

"Oh, that's okay, Jim," said Rob. "I don't know if I mentioned this to you yet, but my mother ate my father a while back, and I still have some unresolved issues around that."

"Uh, gotcha," Jim said, trying to hide his

bewilderment. "Well, anyway, I guess this is good-bye, Rob."

Caught off guard, Rob floated over to Jim, studying the Trollhunter's soot- and slime-streaked face to see if he was joking.

"But-but-but, we're partners," Rob whined. "We ride together until the commissioner throws us into lockup for being a couple of loose cannons!"

Jim kept walking, saying nothing.

"Besides, we had a deal!" Rob added. "I lead you through the Darklands, and you take me back to the surface world for the greatest *Gun Robot* movie marathon since Action Con '87!"

"Only you didn't lead me anywhere," Jim finally said. "And things have changed."

Jim reached a high outcropping of rock and looked out past Madness Canyon. Beyond the labyrinth below him, he saw the remains of Skarlagk's fortress, miles away. Even from here, Jim could see the Horde picking at the broken citadel like a carcass. Oily black fumes drifted from its spire like a lopsided chimney, blotting out the Darklands' photo-negative sun.

"Everything's changed," said Jim, his grim stare

still fixed on what was left of Skarlagk's rebellion. "The deal's off."

"No it ISN'T," Jim heard Rob say, the Heetling's voice building with each word.

Turning around, Jim saw Rob's flames burning brighter than ever, his face screwed up in anger, before he reverted into his fireball shape.

"HOW DARE YOU?" Rob demanded. "HOW DARE YOU?!"

A great peal of flame arced forth from the fireball, streaking toward Jim. The Trollhunter summoned his shield and endured the blast, gnashing his teeth under the heat. Once the fusillade dissipated, Jim pivoted and smacked Rob away with the flat of his sword.

"How dare *I*?" Jim asked, incredulous, as the fireball's trajectory sent it bouncing off the ground. "Are you *serious*? Can you think about anyone other than yourself for even a second? What about those babies that are trapped a world away from their families?"

Jim gestured with his sword back toward the charred husk of the fortress and said, "What about Skarlagk and her rebels? They may not have been the friendliest bunch, but even they didn't deserve what happened to them!"

"It's like I told ya, rookie," the fireball said as it started to go supernova. "The only way to survive the Darklands is by killing everything else in the Darklands."

Rob flew in a wide path around Jim, trailing fire as he went. Coming full circle, Rob joined one end of the flames to the other, creating a blazing ring around the two of them.

"Stay here long enough, and this place will taint you, too," Rob added.

Jim looked up at the white-hot conflagration surrounding him, its continuous wall of fire reaching way over his head. With no way to jump over or through the inferno, the Trollhunter raised his sword and faced his enemy. The unbearable heat kicked up swirling currents of ash and grit between them.

"Tell me where the portal is, partner," said Rob. "Point me to the way out, and I'll point you to the nursery."

Jim squinted, skeptical, and said, "I don't believe you. You don't know where it is. You don't know where anything is. You're just some hyperactive liar who's watched *way* too many eighties action movies."

"C'mon," Rob added quickly, as if he hadn't heard any of what Jim just said. "Where'd you leave Killahead Bridge? Tell me. Tell me! TELL ME!"

Jim kept quiet. All he could hear was the beating of his own heart, the sounds of trailing embers scorching his armor, and a nearby shriek. The fireball stared like an unblinking eye.

"Okay," Jim began. "The portal . . . it . . . it's in the maze."

"See?" said Rob cheerfully as he turned back into his humanoid shape. "Was that so hard? And the maze, huh? Clever! You must've just walked out of there right before I met you."

"Yep," Jim replied. "And now you'll show me where Enrique is?"

Rob shrugged his lit shoulders and said, "Oh yeah, about that . . . see, that was a double cross. It's a staple of any action flick, as is a killer catchphrase. Like this one: 'Gun Robot is gunning for YOU, Doctor Despot!'"

Rob reverted back into a ball and opened fire

on Jim—literally. But the Trollhunter saw it coming and jumped out of the way. The blasts hit the black sand where Jim had just stood, fusing it into a patch of glass. Jim ran toward the fireball and engaged his shield again before jumping. The Trollhunter landed shield-first on top of Rob and pushed himself off the floating orb in a single springing motion. The momentum carried Jim high into the air and over the ring of fire.

He landed clear of the flames on the other side, detached the shield from his gauntlet, and used it to surf down the canyon wall. The sky erupted with flames behind Jim as Rob flew after him. Skidding to a halt at the bottom of Madness Canyon, Jim made a break for the maze dead ahead of him.

"You can't lose me in there!" Rob called after Jim. "I'll find you and cook you like a canned ham in your armor!"

Jim zigged and zagged through the labyrinth, trying to put distance between himself and the fireball. But Rob's voice echoed through the maze.

"Then I'll use your portal to get to the surface and buy a matinee ticket at the closest movie theater! And then I'll burn your entire world! But not the movie theater! That place I'll leave alone!"

Running deeper and deeper into the maze, Jim finally stopped. He had reached a hub from which multiple pathways branched into different directions, like the spokes of a wheel.

"WHERE ARE YOU?" shouted the fireball from nearby. "WHERE ARE YOU??"

His breath ragged from exhaustion, Jim dropped to his knees in front of a cluster of rocks. The labyrinth lit up around him as Rob tracked Jim into the hub.

"Can you feel it?" Rob asked.

Jim remained kneeling, not looking back at Rob. Instead, he glanced to either side, as if waiting for something. Sweat dripped from the tip of his nose, splashing on the round, red rocks below him.

"The electric guitars in the rock 'n' roll score are starting to play," Rob went on. "The chopper is hovering overhead, and the police cars are racing to the docks of Long Beach Harbor. This is the end of our story, partner."

"Do I get a final speech?" Jim asked, still on the ground.

He pressed his hands to the labyrinth floor and

felt a vibration build under him. Rob, floating in the air, didn't seem to notice.

"I guess," Rob said after thinking it over. "But could you do it with Spanish subtitles for our Latin American audiences?"

"I'll do you one better," said Jim as he stood up. "I'll give you the one part of the movie that you forgot."

"Forgot?" Rob repeated in bewilderment, oblivious to the mounting vibrations beneath his round, levitating form. "What did I leave out?"

"The part right before the very end," Jim said, his body tensing in anticipation. "When the good guy walks away, and the bad guy gets back up one final time."

"Oh, you mean the last-minute jump scare!" Rob answered before a deafening shriek split the air.

Several more screeches followed as countless Nyarlagroths snaked out of the passageways surrounding the hub. Jim quickly moved away from the round, red, rocky Nyarlagroth eggs that had been by his knees.

"You tricked me!" Rob cried. "But the trick's on you! I can just fly outta here!"

The fireball started to zoom away, but Jim recalled his whips into his hands and unfurled them into the air. He wrapped them around Rob and held him fast in place, just as they had done with the Helheetis from the Horde.

"No, you can't," said Jim.

The Nyarlagroths all ignored the Trollhunter, focusing instead on the bound sphere of fire shining above them. The sight reminded Jim of the moths he and his mom would sometimes see gathered around their porch lights. Rob struggled to pull free as several sets of teeth nipped and snapped at him, but the whips remained taut.

"NO!" screamed Rob. "You can't do this! You'll never defeat me! I'll see you again! I'll see you—AT THE MOVIES!"

He shot streams of fire at the eels, which puffed harmlessly against their durable hides.

"Nyarlagroths are fireproof on the outside," Jim reminded him.

Their lips peeled back in hunger. Their jaws scissored open. And then the largest of the Nyarlagroths ate Rob in a single clapping bite.

"And the inside," said Jim before he made his

whips fade into nothingness.

The other eels turned on the largest, greedily attacking it for the bright thing it had just swallowed. The Trollhunter used the distraction to slip away undetected. As he departed the hub, Jim could still hear Rob's muffled voice from somewhere inside the Nyarlagroth's digestive tract. Only the fireball wasn't talking. He was *singing*.

"This robot's heart has been programmed for loooove," crooned Rob. "Hate does not compute, because you're supercute. We go together, like a metal hand in a glooooove. . . ."

CHAPTER 18
DRAWN TOGETHER

Jim removed the emerald gem from his chest plate and tossed it into the placid black lake he had found. He didn't know how long it had taken him to get out of the labyrinth. Minutes, hours, days—in a land without a sunrise, time blurred together into one long nightmare. But in that time, something Rob said lingered with Jim.

Stay here long enough, and this place will taint you, too.

As much as Jim hated to admit it, this was probably the one true thing Rob had ever told him in their brief, chaotic time together. So, when Jim finally exited the maze and found the undisturbed body of water, he was all too happy to get rid of the gem and the whips it had created in his armor.

Jim waded into the lake and sniffed it. It smelled overwhelmingly of sulfur, but seemed otherwise harmless. Cupping the fetid water in his hands, Jim washed away the grime that coated his skin and armor. He caught his rippling reflection and realized he hadn't seen his own face in the longest time. Jim barely recognized the pale, gaunt, and weary person that stared back at him.

Exiting the lake, Jim retraced his steps and came upon the spot where he had cut his way free of that Nyarlagroth's belly. Jim retrieved Skarlagk's satchel from the blob of partially digested muck that followed him out of the creature's guts. He opened it and found a few more of those gross bladder canteens, as well as the nub of chalk Skarlagk used to draw her maps.

She had a violent way of doing things, Jim thought. *But Skarlagk did sorta save my life.*

He took her satchel and a length of chain that had also been in the eel's stomach and walked over to a barren ravine. Along the way, he couldn't help but think more about Skarlagk. Yes, she had spared him from encountering one monster by tossing Jim inside of another. But Jim wondered if he had maybe saved Skarlagk, in a way, before the end. That last look he saw in her eyes—when she had let go of the revenge that so fueled her life—somehow warmed Jim. He supposed that was maybe how Skarlagk used to look ages ago, when she, too, was sixteen.

Reaching the ravine, Jim anchored the chain around a jagged tusk of rock and climbed down to the ledge. He let the chain hang there, pulled the chalk from the satchel, and marked a white arrow on the wall to keep track of his location. Jim continued along the edge, until he found a recessed alcove that offered privacy and protection. He sank to the alcove floor, his arms and legs aching from overuse.

As he sat there, alone, Jim thought again of those moths by the porch light. That memory was the first time he had allowed himself to think of his mom in days. Pretty soon, AAARRRGGHH!!!, Blinky, Draal, NotEnrique, and especially Toby and Claire flooded back into Jim's mind. He had tried so hard to keep from remembering his friends—from missing them—because he thought that was the key to surviving the Darklands.

"But maybe I should've been doing the opposite," Jim said to himself, his voice thick with emotion.

Now that the floodgates were open, Jim didn't want to stop thinking of everyone back home. He wanted to see them more than ever. Looking down, Jim found the chalk still in his hand. Inspiration struck him, and he began sketching his extended human and Troll family on the alcove's slate walls. Jim never thought he was much of an artist, but his mom once told him how she used to paint before he was born.

Losing himself in the chalk, Jim didn't stop until he had finished rendering Claire, Toby, Blinky, and AAARRRGGHH!!! All of a sudden, he didn't feel so alone. All of a sudden, that hollowness inside his chest went away.

All of a sudden, the Trollhunter smiled.

EPILOGUE
A LIFE OF ALMOST DEAD . . .

Being Jim was not fun.

Toby reached this conclusion in the days after he had returned from the Kelpestrum with the Glamour Mask. Toby had donned the mask and assumed Jim's form mere seconds before Barbara woke from her extended nap. Now that the effects of the memory charm had worn off, Barbara felt more alert than she had in days. And Toby's impression of Jim was serviceable enough—certainly better than Blinky's—that Barbara believed he really was her son.

But the pride Toby felt in successfully imitating his best friend turned to guilt when Barbara gave "Jim" a kiss on the cheek. In that moment, he felt more like an impostor. That said, he figured this charade was better for Jim's mom than learning the truth about what had happened to her *real* son.

Claire didn't have much of an easier go of it, either. With Toby keeping up appearances in Jim's home life, she covered for Jim at school. But since she couldn't pretend to be Jim in class without being marked absent herself, Claire had to get creative.

Thus was born Jim Lake Disease. The rumor that Jim was quarantined at the hospital with an ultrarare condition had spread through the school hallways like, well, a virus. Claire also felt guilty. She hated the idea of making up a phony disease while there were so many genuinely sick people in the world. But Claire also understood that people generally avoided talking about the uncomfortable subject of illness. And anything that kept students and teachers from asking too many questions about Jim was probably a good thing, as far as Claire was concerned.

So, she created a fake web page detailing Jim Lake Disease, handed Eli Pepperjack a coin collection can, and acted sad whenever anyone mentioned Jim's name. Only it wasn't much of an act for Claire. All she could do was donate the money Eli collected to *actual* charities and hope that each new day would bring Jim back to her.

Blinky tried to keep himself busy as well. As Draal and a reluctant NotEnrique pitched in on the rebuilding efforts in Trollmarket, the six-eyed Troll remained in his library. He tinkered with Toby's Warhammer, trying to devise a way to make it telescope down in size like Claire's Shadow Staff. And whenever he took a break from that, Blinky would just hit the books and search in vain for a way into the Darklands.

After closing what felt like the millionth useless scroll, Blinky rubbed his bleary eyes and stared at AAARRRGGHH!!!'s stone body in the corner.

"I really miss him, AAARRRGGHH!!!" Blinky said. "I miss you both."

Miss you, too, AAARRRGGHH!!! wanted to say back to Blinky.

But the words never seemed to leave the foggy borderlands between life and death, in which AAARRRGGHH!!! had spent the last weeks. He first woke up here the instant after the Creeper's Sun poison finished turning him to stone. AAARRRGGHH!!!

had then walked around the endless space, hearing everything his friends said around his petrified body, yet unable to make his replies heard.

Little did AAARRRGGHH!!! know that he had actually found an audience in a separate, even more remote dimension. For in the ghostly realm known as the Void, the Council of Trollhunters watched AAARRRGGHH!!!'s roaming spirit.

"Ah, Aarghaumont," said Kanjigar the Courageous. "How good it is to see you, my old friend, even in circumstances such as these."

Kanjigar turned to the other fallen Trollhunters who joined him in observing AAARRRGGHH!!! through a circular window of magic. In all, there were scores of other armored Trolls who had preceded Kanjigar—and now Jim—as Merlin's former champions.

"Although he does not yet realize it, AAARRRGGHH!!! shall be the key to James Lake Junior's salvation," Kanjigar announced.

"How can you be so certain?" squeaked Unkar the Unfortunate. "No other Trollhunter has ever dared to venture into the Darklands. Who's to say he even *can* get out? If he survives, that is!"

"Kanjigar speaks the truth," said Deya the Deliverer, her transparent eyes flashing the same shade of blue as her Amulet. "The Void has shown us both visions of the future. The current Trollhunter will find the child he seeks. He will face Gunmar, and he will escape the Darklands, although not in any way he or his allies could ever expect."

"And this Krubera," began Spar the Spiteful, indicating AAARRRGGHH!!! in the window with his tusks. "He plays some part in the Trollhunter's victory?"

"The Troll is the key," Kanjigar confirmed, his eyes now glowing, too, as the Void gave him another glimpse of tomorrow.

"The key to the Hunter," added Boraz the Bold, his eyes filled with the same future-sight.

"The Troll is the key," said Gogun the Gentle, eyes aglow.

"The key to the Hunter," repeated Tellad-Urr the Terrible.

Soon, the entire Council of Trollhunters fell into the chant.

The Troll is the key, the key to the Hunter.

Kanjigar was the last to join in the spectral

chorus, for he had seen something else in the latest vision the Void had shared.

The Troll is the key, the key to the Hunter.

AAARRRGGHH!!! would indeed prove crucial to rescuing the human Trollhunter from the Darklands—as would Kanjigar, in his own way.

The Troll is the key, the key to the Hunter.

And that's when Jim Lake Jr. would face his greatest challenge yet.

READ ON FOR MORE

DREAMWORKS

TROLLHUNTERS
TALES OF ARCADIA
FROM GUILLERMO DEL TORO

Ready to embark on another exciting
Arcadian adventure with the Trollhunters?
Here's a sneak peek at **AGE OF THE AMULET.**

Once the Horngazel tunnel closed behind him,
Tellad-Urr let out a long, calming breath. He found
himself on a grassy field on the surface world, sur-
rounded by the ring of standing stone pillars he had
erected during his rare downtime. *Stonehenge*, the
humans had taken to calling it. The Trollhunter
looked up at the sky. The sun had not yet risen, but
it colored the horizon a deep shade of red. Red as
flame. Red as blood.

In an existence filled with duty and discipline,
this sight was the only thing that brought The
Trollhunter a sense of relief—although he always

had to leave right before the sunrise, lest his Troll body be turned to solid rock. Tellad-Urr sighed . . . before a familiar blue glow flashed in his eyes. The Amulet shone in the grass before him. He seized the device and said, "I hate you."

"Finally," came a grim voice behind him. "Something we agree upon."

Tellad-Urr spun around. From the shadows of Stonehenge, a powerfully large Gumm-Gumm emerged, his fangs plainly visible in the overbite formed by his mismatched jaws.

"Orlagk the Oppressor," said Tellad-Urr. "Have you come to finally surrender your Gumm-Gumm army? Or are you here for another pointless battle?"

"My forces shall never surrender, Trollhunter," said Orlagk. "Even now, they train with my most brutal general, Gunmar. And as for battle, I assure you . . ."

The Gumm-Gumm flexed his claw, forcing strands of opaque energy to rise and weave into the jagged shape of a sword. Once it had solidified, Orlagk trained his Decimaar Blade on Tellad-Urr and said, "This one has a point."

RICHARD ASHLEY HAMILTON

is best known for his storytelling across DreamWorks Animation's How to Train Your Dragon franchise, having written for the Emmy-nominated Dream-Works *Dragons: Race to the Edge* on Netflix and the official DreamWorks Dragons expanded universe bible. In his heart, Richard remains a lifelong comic book fan and has written and developed numerous titles, including *Trollhunters: The Secret History of Trollkind* (with Marc Guggenheim) for Dark Horse Comics and his original series *Scoop* for Insight Editions. Richard lives in Silver Lake, California, with his wife and their two sons.